Parsifal

Parsifal

a novel

by Jim Krusoe

 TIN HOUSE BOOKS / Portland, Oregon & New York, New York

Published by Tin House Books, Portland, Oregon, and New York, New York

Distributed to the trade by Publishers Group West, 1700 Fourth St., Berkeley, CA 94710, www.pgw.com

Library of Congress Cataloging-in-Publication Data
Krusoe, James.
 Parsifal : a novel / by Jim Krusoe. — 1st U.S. ed.
    p. cm.
 ISBN 978-1-935639-34-3 (trade paper) — ISBN 978-1-935639-35-0 (ebook)
 I. Title.
 PS3561.R873P37 2012
 813'.54—dc23
                                    2012002837

Grateful acknowledgment is made to Sony/ATV Music for permission to reprint lyrics from "I'm So Lonesome I Could Cry," by Hank Williams, ©1949 Sony/ATV Music Publishing LLC. All rights administered by Sony/ATV Music Publishing LLC, 8 Music Square West, Nashville, TN 37203. All rights reserved. Used by permission.

First U.S. edition 2012
Printed in the USA
Interior design by Jakob Vala

www.tinhouse.com

For Henry

Il pleure dans mon coeur
Comme il pleut sur la ville.
Quelle est cette langueur
Qui pénêtre mon coeur?

It rains in my heart
As it rains on the town
What is this sadness
That creeps into my heart?
—Verlaine

I

here is a war between the earth and sky.

Also, there are monsters.

Parsifal thinks he may be one of them.

Parsifal is of average height, and more or less normal looking, except for the scar.

One day Parsifal stood on the sidewalk outside his house, not looking at the sidewalk, which was an ordinary sidewalk, and not even looking at his feet, which

were ordinary as well. Instead, Parsifal looked upward
at a bird turning in circles, or slow spirals.

The bird made no discernible sound, while all around
him Parsifal could hear car doors slam, traffic move, even
the tapping cane of a blind man as the man walked toward him. (Parsifal lived near a center for the blind whose
patrons often used the sidewalks of his neighborhood
for practice.) Although the bird was very high, Parsifal
imagined he could describe the exact sound of the wind
as it passed over the bird's feathers. He imagined it was
the sound of the ocean, the same sound he sometimes
heard when he picked up a seashell and held it to his ear.

Parsifal had been raised in the forest.

A librarian Parsifal once knew told him she believed
that monsters were monsters only because they enjoyed
being monsters, and it was this pleasure, not any scales
or claws or fangs or actual acts a monster might com-
mit, that made people fear them.

Parsifal thinks about this often.

Parsifal's first idea was that the bird was an albatross.
All he knew from watching it, however, was that it was
a large bird of some kind, moving in spirals, or circles,
the center of which seemed to be his own head.

Then there is also the sand, and there is the lightning.

When Joe asked Parsifal which one he preferred he answered: the sand.

Most people agree it sometimes hurts to think about a thing for too long, and whenever this is about to happen, it is a good idea for that person to look away.

But at the same time, the things a person needs to look away from are often the most important things to think about.

What do people mean by "a war between the earth and sky"? They mean this: that lately and, in fact, quite frequently, objects have been falling out of the sky—mostly car parts, but other objects as well, like microwave ovens, for example—and when one of them strikes the earth, it can make a crater and harm people, too. It does not appear the falling objects are aimed at humans in particular, and this provides a certain degree of comfort, but at the same time it must be said that because so many things are falling, some loss of life is to be expected.

The earth, on its part, fights back by throwing into the sky eruptions from volcanoes and smoke from forest fires. Sometimes it makes sandstorms, too.

And between the earth and the sky, which one does Parsifal want to win?

He considers the question.

Once when Parsifal was talking with a different librarian, she said to him: "But no one said anything about killing."

This librarian and Parsifal had been intimate only moments earlier, and were lying on her bed, one that had a canopy of green and blue cloth, so that lying there was like looking through leaves at the sky. On that exact occasion, however, Parsifal and the librarian were not looking at the canopy; they were staring out the sliding glass door of her bedroom and watching the thick, surprisingly dark smoke of a distant forest fire fill the sky with ash.

In fact, Parsifal was certain she was right—that no one *had* said anything about killing—and he wondered why she had brought it up, but just as he was about to agree, he remembered what his mother used to tell him.

"Hold your tongue," Parsifal's mother used to say, "or the bear will bite it off."

minimum wage, and the man would receive the same amount of money whether he collected a thousand dollars or nothing. This man would be paid in cash, in an envelope, at the end of the day. Parsifal also knew that people in this line of work would sometimes put a little money aside for themselves, and who could blame them? Not that Parsifal was saying this particular man did such a thing, of course, but many people did, and to accomplish it they usually enlisted an accomplice to visit them before their shift ended, so they could hand that person whatever money they wished to "siphon off" before they were checked at the end of the day by their supervisors. Then after work the two would meet up in a bar, where the confederate would return the money that he had been given a few hours earlier, minus his commission. Parsifal could not be sure if this man was blind or if he was only wearing dark glasses.

But whether he was blind or not, Parsifal was sure the man had the face of a person who had been responsible for much pain to others in his lifetime and would no doubt cause more before he died. Also, the red lettering beneath the pictures seemed angry, as if the man himself had drawn them for no other reason than to take money away from people who needed it more than the man did, especially because the total amount the man turned in each day made no difference to him personally. Unless the man was stealing, of course. Plus, if the man had drawn the pictures himself it would mean he wasn't blind, although Parsifal had to admit the man had never claimed to be blind.

"You," this man had said to Parsifal, "how would you like to donate a little something to help these needy children?"

"No thank you," Parsifal told him. "Because I doubt more than ten or twenty percent of your total take for the day will ever see these so-called children after you and your managers take your cut."

Then the man stood up from behind his table as if he were going to jump out and hit Parsifal. "Get out of here, you cheap bastard," he said.

So Parsifal knew then he had been correct, that this man was an angry man, a man just looking to start a fight.

Some people say that the first Parsifal, Parsifal's namesake, wasted his whole life in search of a cup with the power to heal all wounds, but according to others there never was a cup to be found—only a black stone that had fallen from the sky.

Furthermore, there is a difference of opinion over whether he ever found it or not.

Lightning or sand?

"The sand," Parsifal told Joe.

Parsifal's first girlfriend, a librarian, once asked him this: "Have you ever considered that the reason people dream is so they won't have to believe the rest of life is all there is?" They were in her bedroom, a different bedroom from the one of the librarian he watched the forest fire with, and so the bed was different, too. There was no canopy, for one thing, and also this bedroom had no sliding doors. Plus it was night, so even if there had been smoke they couldn't have seen it. Then she asked him if he ever dreamed, and as she waited for an answer she stood naked in front of the mirrored doors covering her closet. She raised her arms above her head and then slowly lowered them.

"The only dreams I have," Parsifal told her at last, "are those in which I die."

"You poor man," she said.

Her name was Trellis, and she was the same librarian who had brought up the subject of monsters.

Another time, when Parsifal and Trellis were standing outside a bakery trying to decide whether to go in, she told him she had read that blindness was a condition at least as much psychological as physical. "I'm not saying that those blind people have themselves to blame, but it's something to consider," she said, and Parsifal watched as her reflection in the window mixed in with the pies and cakes and cookies that lay behind it.

"Where did you read that?" he asked, because he wanted to know more, but Trellis claimed she had forgotten.

On yet another occasion Trellis told him that certain animals were able to smell death months, or even years, before it arrived.

Another time, while waiting for a completely different librarian to finish her shift, Parsifal sat at a library table and read an article about a woman called Mother Teresa. According to the article, Mother Teresa used to say, "God in His infinite wisdom will provide for his children."

This woman, Mother Teresa, ran a hospital that was so crowded with dying patients that they had to sleep in chairs and on the floor, and sometimes, in her hurry to reach a person who was about to die any second, Mother Teresa would accidentally step on a dying person's arm or finger.

"I'm so sorry," she would tell the injured person at those times. "I'm afraid it can't be helped."

There were two theories on how the objects got into the sky. The first was that the awesome power of the wind would draw these objects upward, and then, when the sky was ready, they would be released back to earth.

The second theory was that certain unscrupulous humans were somehow in league with the sky—for financial reasons, no doubt—and, by means of silent aircraft or balloons, carried these objects up into the air to drop them.

These two ideas were essentially all anyone had to offer about the situation.

Entrar.

To enter.

On Parsifal's first trip to the ocean he watched two boys, about four and eight, play a game with their dog. The dog was small—a mix with short legs, a silky blond coat, and black protruding eyes. Because in his forest there were only foxes and the like, the ways of dogs were still mostly unknown to Parsifal.

The game consisted of the children dragging the dog into the waves by means of a rope attached to its neck so it would be knocked over and try to get up. Then the dog would be knocked down again by another wave. The waves weren't large, but were large enough to knock over a small dog, and when by chance the dog made it back to the shore, the boys would pull it in again. The boys appeared to be brothers.

Eventually the dog stopped struggling. It lay still as the water washed back and forth over and around it, moving its fine hair, lifting its body ever so slightly and then dropping it again onto the sand. When the dog finally drowned, the brothers began to leave, but then one of them, the older and more responsible, remembered the rope, so he returned and untied it from the dog and took it back home.

In the forest Parsifal had lived primarily on fungus, moss, and slugs—things of the earth, his mother called them—but also they ate eggs, and sometimes Parsifal would bring home a dead squirrel or raccoon, which they would eat as well. Because in the forest things break more rapidly than in other places, Parsifal and his mother, Pearl, were forced to work every day repairing their simple hovel. Later, when he was old enough, it became his job to carry long strips of bark up to the roof in order to replace those pieces that had blown off during the night.

In the forest scarcely a day went by that Parsifal did not receive a bruise, or cut, or rash from some unusual and deadly species of plant or insect, not to mention scrapes and plenty of sprained ankles from tripping over roots, because Parsifal's ankles weren't the greatest. Surprisingly often, a branch would drop onto his head without warning, so afterward he would have to lie on a bed of leaves looking at the canopy of the sky until he had regained enough balance to walk safely back home again.

A monster.

Back when Parsifal lived in the forest, not much seemed to be falling out of the sky. Or it may have been that things *were* falling, but the thick, green canopy of trees deflected them. Or it may have been that the canopy did not deflect anything so much as muffle the sounds of the falling objects, so the only objects he could hear were those that fell extremely close by, and they—as mentioned earlier—were mostly branches.

Once when Parsifal was lying in the completely ordinary bed of yet one more librarian, after having made love, she sighed. "Parsifal," she said, "you have a big name to live up to, but I'd say you do pretty well."

"Huh?" he said.

"I mean," she said, "a child raised in the forest among animals."

"That's not exactly true," Parsifal said. "There was also my mother."

This same librarian wrote down for Parsifal a definition of a monster: *a deformed or oversized creature frequently dangerous to men.*

"The silence of a falling star."

Pearl used to sing that.

One day long after Parsifal left the forest and had settled down in the city (by then having started his business of repairing fountain pens), he was in the process of replacing the sac on an old Eversharp when there was a knock on the door of his house. When he opened his door, there stood the most beautiful woman he had ever seen outside of various photos of beautiful women or those in paintings in museums. In fact, this woman was more beautiful than many in paintings because museums do not choose paintings for the beauty of their subjects, but for their craft and for the brilliance of their execution.

So this woman stood at Parsifal's door holding a Lady Waterman pen with gold trim, and the barrel of the pen seemed to be in good shape except for a little scuffing where the cap had been posted.

She said to Parsifal, "I heard you fix fountain pens."

Fortunately, he was not at a loss for words. He waved the Eversharp he was holding (it was in two sections at that moment) and said, "It appears that you've come to the right place."

"It appears I have," she said.

When he remembers that time by the ocean, Parsifal decides that the children's father would probably have been angry if they had returned home having forgotten the rope and would have beaten the boys for losing it.

"My name is Misty," the beautiful woman said.

"Misty," Parsifal replied.

"Yes," she answered. "My parents told me they named me that because I was conceived in an unusually heavy fog, one that blanketed the entire coast where they had gone for a vacation. It lasted nearly a week, during which time driving, even walking, was considered too dangerous for anyone to attempt, so they decided to be intimate instead."

Misty grimaced as if the memory was somehow disturbing, and added that the ink flow of the Waterman was inadequate for her needs.

Then Parsifal told her he could not be certain whether the problem lay in the feed itself, in some problem with the seating of the nib, or even in the flexibility of the sac, without first taking the pen apart for an examination. "Can you leave it for a day or two?" he asked.

"Yes, I can," she answered.

Frequently Parsifal would ask himself what other kind of bird besides an albatross made such large circles in the sky. Or maybe they were spirals. He was no expert in these matters, to be sure, but he thought it could also have been a hawk or an eagle. Even a vulture.

"His infinite wisdom," Parsifal remembers Mother Teresa having said.

Back when he was still living in his house in the forest (not even a house, really, but more an accumulation of branches into which his mother and he crawled each night), Parsifal opened the door (how an actual door had come to be there was a complicated story) to find a bear inside. The bear was an ordinary black bear, though with a white spot on its chest, and of medium size, similar to many others that lived alongside them in the forest, mostly harmless to humans, but once inside their house—which was only a single room—the bear had eaten a dozen eggs his mother had been saving for dinner, as well as the pet squirrel that Parsifal had raised from a baby and had not yet gotten around to naming.

Basically there are four kinds of pens if you do not count dip pens, which Parsifal does not, because it is his opinion that dip pens are really not much more than pointed sticks. The kinds of pens are Cartridge, Sac, Piston, and Eyedropper. Of this list, he feels the most reprehensible is the cartridge, because it is nothing more than a prepackaged tube of ink, on to one end of which a person adds a pointed stick. And even though some cartridges you can squeeze and then release, forcing them to suck ink inside, which is the way a sac works, and other cartridges are made to work like a piston, in the end a cartridge is neither a sac nor a piston, but only a cheap piece of plastic crap, and if a person chooses to believe otherwise he or she is fooling no one but him- or herself.

Entrar.

Which librarian told him about the opera *Parsifal* he can't remember, only that he was with her in her kitchen, which smelled of cinnamon and lavender, and she was using her oven to heat up a coffee cake with crumbs on top. Whoever it was, that person told him the opera was essentially about a young man who achieves enlightenment in one way or another.

"Maybe that's what's on deck for you," she added. "You never can tell."

"Lights up a purple sky," Pearl used to sing.

The next type is the sac, which is more or less a balloon with ink. A sac fills by being squeezed shut by a lever, or by fingers, or by something else, and then released. "Think of a baster for a Thanksgiving turkey," Parsifal likes to say, "but with a metal point at the end to write with, and you are thinking of a pen with a sac." Would you want to compose an intimate letter with a turkey baster?

Parsifal would not.

Eyedropper pens really are nothing more than hollow tubes that people fill with ink by using an eyedropper to transfer the ink from the bottle to the pen—the same type of eyedropper people use to put drops in their noses or ears or eyes, and which really is just a miniature turkey baster.

Thus for Parsifal, the only true pen is one in which the ink-holding mechanism is not auxiliary to the pen, but *a part of the pen itself*: the piston type. In the piston type, the piston built into the pen sucks up ink on its own—and also expels it, if needed. Where other pens are passive, the piston is active. "Think of a squid moving along the floor of the ocean in darkness and silence by means of taking in and expelling seawater," Parsifal says. That would be a *piston pen*, only substitute ink for seawater, though come to think of it, a squid has ink as well—and uses it to hide.

If only he could hide, he sometimes thinks, and then, when everything has passed, come out again.

But what is *everything*?

The Lady Waterman looked as if it needed a good cleaning. It used a sac and not a piston, but sometimes, as Parsifal had learned the hard way, if a person wanted to stay in business, it was necessary to compromise his ideals.

To enter.

Meanwhile, in response to the increased bombardment from the sky, the earth seems more intent than ever on filling the sky with particles of ash and smoke. In other words, it appears that the earth is bent on replacing particles of the air with particles of itself by activating more volcanoes and setting more forest fires, some of the latter stretching for miles. If this method proves successful, eventually the air will no longer exist, Parsifal thinks. Instead of air, it will be a half-air-and-half-earth mixture. If this happens, then the sky will be as much like earth as the earth itself and no longer the sky at all. If this happens, then the earth will have won.

"You know what happens to a little boy who asks too many questions, don't you?" Parsifal's mother used to say. "The bear will bite his tongue off. You remember your squirrel, don't you, what's-its-name?"

He thinks: *to enter the forest.*

II

f there was a door between the earth and the sky, what would it look like?

Naturally, there is no reason such a portal would be an ordinary door or resemble, for example, the door to Parsifal's house in the forest. The door to Parsifal's house there was made of oak, had four panels, a heavy latch, a doorknob, and a brass knocker that was pointless because, as his mother used to say, you could hear anyone coming for miles by the sound of snapping twigs. So the door between the earth and the sky would not have to be a door like that door at all. It could be a flap, the kind of a flap used to let pets in and out of a house, or a tube to crawl through, like the escape hatch of a submarine, and the truth is, because no one has ever discovered a door between the earth and the sky, there is no reason it has to look like a door at all. It could have a different shape entirely: a plant, for example, or a leaf, or a cup, even a bird, an animal, or a person.

As much as his mother pretended to admire it, the door to Parsifal's house in the forest was heavy and difficult to open. This was because instead of it being attached by hinges, as most doors in most homes are, Parsifal's father had drilled holes along one side of it and passed through them vines and a few pieces of rope, which he tied to a tree trunk. In fact, the two of them—the son and the mother—seldom opened the door, but most often entered the house instead through a tunnel they had dug beneath the door.

The tunnel collected a considerable amount of water during the rainy season, making it uncomfortable to pass through, forcing them to hold their breaths then, though never for too long.

Parsifal's father was a stockbroker in the city. He seldom came to visit, but when he did, he made it a point to use the door and never the tunnel. His name was Conrad, which means "trusted advisor."

It was while still in the forest that Parsifal constructed his first fountain pen. It consisted of only a seed pod from which the seeds had been removed and replaced with berry juice. He snipped off one end of the pod, brown and dry at that moment, and let the juice flow out onto the face of a large sycamore leaf that was spread out on a stump.

First he wrote his name: *Parsifal.*

And next he wrote: *I want to die.*

That last part just came out.

"Good handwriting is a lovely thing to have, especially for a boy your age," Parsifal's mother said, "but I wonder if you've ever thought about the fact that all handwriting, good or bad, is only a form of the ultimate writing, and that somewhere, as fine as your Ws and your Ds may be, there exists a completely perfect W, and a perfect D as well, letters that will make your own attempts (and everyone else's, for that matter) seem pathetic and laughable by comparison. Perhaps one day you will find them, the perfect W and D, but I doubt it. Nonetheless, it only matters that you try, my son, because all searches are the same search."

They were sitting on a big oak log, and, possibly because they both were still, by the time she finished her speech Parsifal was not surprised to see a large forest rattlesnake crawl out from beneath a rock where it had been sleeping and stop in a little patch of moss at their feet. The snake paused and put out its forked tongue a few times to test the air. It made almost no sound. Parsifal's mother did not even notice it, thinking about handwriting as she probably was.

Losing no time, her son wrenched a limb from the rotting log and smashed it into the unfortunate snake's head, killing it instantly.

"You didn't have to do that," Pearl said.

Because the forest had created his scars, as long as Parsifal stayed in the forest the scars were part of the forest. It was only when he left the forest that they became actual scars.

He could not help but notice that as Misty handed him the Lady Waterman, she looked away, avoiding the sight of his face.

Lately, not only had the quantity of things falling from the sky started to increase—someone or something had gotten hold of a fresh lot of auto parts—but also, increasingly, objects had begun hitting humans to a degree that seemed far more than coincidental. An engine block, for example, fell through the roof of a classroom used for people to learn English as a second language, and shortly after that, seven senior citizens practicing tai chi in a local park were picked off one by one by a series of falling Chevrolet water pumps.

This second event was on the local news: emergency vehicles waiting on the street, four old women and three old men in comfortable clothing, their inert forms lying on the grass, several with horrible wounds, one of the latter still wearing a straw hat, in the words of the newscaster, "a futile attempt to protect his head from harm coming from above." All around them children played on the swings, people threw Frisbees and walked their dogs, stopping every so often to clean up after them.

A childhood memory: One year in the forest, winter came early and on a morning still at the beginning of autumn, when Parsifal tried to leave his house via the tunnel beneath the front door, not only had the tunnel filled with water (as was usual), but the surface on the other side of the tunnel, the outside, was covered with ice. Unfortunately

Parsifal learned this after he had already dived down and was forced to use his head to break the frozen surface, leaving a nasty scar at the top of his skull.

Later in the winter, when the same sort of thing kept happening, a person returning home from the outside could always take a stick or rock and bang it hard enough to break the ice. But when leaving the house, or when it got really cold and the water in the tunnel would freeze into a solid block of ice, Parsifal was forced to press all his weight against the heavy door in order to leave his home, and when Pearl had to leave the house she would have Parsifal go first.

The meaning of Pearl is *a smooth, lustrous, round structure inside the shell of a clam or oyster, much valued as a jewel. Usually found in the ocean.*

In one of Parsifal's dreams he is standing on the sidewalk in front of his house in the city when he is struck in the chest by a bullet. He doesn't know who fired it or why, only that he's been hit. In this particular dream, he lives long enough to be sure that he is really dying before he wakes.

Another time he is hiding in the crawl space beneath some building or another because bombs are dropping outside. It's hot and hard to breathe because of all the dust, and there are spiders and other insects, maybe even a rat, along with him as well. Then there is a flash, and without thinking anything about it Parsifal becomes a part of that flash and every molecule of him dissolves into whiteness, without a thought, without words, without him.

Parsifal is also the name of an epic poem in German. "It's kind of a stupid story, really," a librarian who was only there for one day, filling in for another librarian who had the flu, told him, "but a major theme in it is love."

She had red hair, and after she said this she blushed.
"Maybe not so stupid," Parsifal told her.

The only person who had no trouble at all opening the front door, in winter or in summer, was his father, Conrad.

On his visits to the forest, Conrad would bring certificates from defunct stocks, piles of junk bonds with their bright gold lettering, and glossy prospectuses for new offerings. No matter how many he brought, for Parsifal, who had little else to play with besides twigs and leaves, each one was a treasure. His first reading lessons, for example, were from the certificates of a failed industrial-waste-treatment corporation and, after he had grown tired of reading aloud the words "Universal Bonded Sewage," he crumpled the certificates on which the words were printed into little balls to fill his mattress with, because high-quality paper lasted longer than leaves, which tended to be brittle and break apart after only a few nights.

And though one might suppose that such an early exposure to the life-pulse of capitalism might have engendered in Parsifal a love for the world of investment and finance (the world of his father), in fact it had the opposite effect. Reading the prospectuses of so many failed stocks, tracing out the self-incriminating promises of so many failed corporations, made him more wary than enthusiastic. And ironically, although the flat, white surfaces and the fine paper of these certificates *should* have provided the ideal medium for Parsifal to practice his penmanship, for some reason he ignored them all in favor of his usual stationery of leaves, flat rocks, the inside of bark, and, best of all, animal skins.

One day, not long after Parsifal met Misty, it occurred to him that she might very well be the sort of person who owned a camper, the kind of vehicle outfitted with a simple kitchen and a bed that could be used to take trips around the country.

He could not say why he thought this.

Not that the forest was ideal, but forever afterward, whether Parsifal was working to repair a pen or simply sitting in a kitchen chair listening to the tapping of the blind, when he thought of the forest he thought of being a child, of being in that state of mind a child has, and it was that state he wished to retrieve. And of the items Parsifal remembered fondly from the forest, the object that always jumped foremost into his mind was the cup that Conrad made for him. It was formed out of metal, but shallow, and more in fact like a bowl with a handle on one side

into which, by means of a hammer and a nail, his father had pounded the name of the cup itself, *Fenjewla*, in a circle around its sides.

"Here," his father said, "I made this cup for you, and you can use it to drink water from in the summer and eat hot soup from in the winter, though you will have to remember that because the cup is made of metal it transmits heat quickly, and in the case of soup it will be easy to burn your hands."

Conrad was right, though after a couple of times Parsifal got the hang of it, and afterward, as long as he was in the forest, there was not a day he did not use it either to drink water or to hold his soup. Sometimes he would use it to gather birds' eggs, and at others to hold unusual stones that he would bring home and offer to Pearl.

Parsifal loved that cup, and he loved its name, *Fenjewla*, but when he asked his father what it meant, Conrad only smiled and said, "As in the case of your own name, Parsifal, you will learn its meaning soon enough."

And in fact it was that librarian who first told him about his name.

Also, it's true that the whole time Parsifal and Pearl were in the forest they were surrounded by bears, but you have to remember that these bears were relatively small and, except for eating his pet squirrel, shy.

One day, while waiting in the library, Parsifal read: *There is nothing we can do that does not praise, not even dying.*

But praise of what, exactly?

Sometimes he woke in the middle of the night with what his therapist, Joe, described as "a panic attack."

"Is there anything I can do about it?" Parsifal would ask.

"Not much," was Joe's invariable reply.

How Parsifal began to associate the war between the sky and the earth with leaving his former life in the forest, he does not know; he only knows that following Joe's death the conviction grew in him that if he could just reenter the world of his youth and reclaim Fenjewla, things would stop falling from heaven, the earth would stop burning itself up in fires and volcanoes.

And no one was more aware than he that if he'd discussed his plan with Joe, Joe would have called it an "unhealthy primal regression."

But by then Joe had already been dead for quite a while.

"Stick out your hands," Pearl said to him, and he held out his hands. Then his mother took his hands in hers, a finger at a time, holding each one motionless by pressing firmly on its last joint with her left hand as with her right hand she used her steel shears to cut his fingernails. When she had finished, she would sweep the cuttings into a small pile, choose a tree, and together they'd dig a hole at its base, dropping the nail clippings at its bottom.

"In this way," Parsifal's mother told him, "the forest will grow to be a part of you and you will be a part of this forest, even after you leave it, as one day you must."

His mother used these same shears when it came time to cut his hair. First, she ran her hand over his scalp and let his hair crop up between her fingers. Then she cut off anything above that height.

When she cut Parsifal's nails, she was silent, scarcely breathing, but when she cut his hair, she hummed to herself.

"Stick out your tongue," Pearl used to say at unexpected moments, "and the bear will bite it off."

The workbench at Parsifal's pen repair business always gave him a feeling of calm. It was a complete world in itself, one that contained everything anyone could possibly need to face any problem: pliers, nib pullers, section tools, jeweler's loupes, a compact grinding machine, polishing cloths, and a shelf with bottles of ink. That night, as Parsifal dismantled the Lady Waterman, he decided that the sac was not the problem; it was firm and resilient. He decided to soak both the feed and the metal nib in ammonia diluted with water; it was a simple trick, but one that solved a variety of problems. Then he went to bed and did not dream at all.

In the morning, Parsifal rinsed the assembly several times with plain water and then replaced the feed and the nib, making sure the nib was centered and not too tight. He drew a little Scrip blue ink into the sac to try it out; it worked beautifully. As a bonus, he smoothed the tip just a little and rubbed polish into a scratch or two along the barrel. *The pen looks good*, he thought, *I wonder if Misty will remark about the difference?* He called the number she had given him and left a message on her answering machine.

"Your pen is ready and waiting," Parsifal told her.

Sand. Parsifal had answered.

One of the first things Parsifal noticed was that the blind men who walked around his block tended to wear light-colored or neutral clothing, avoiding bright reds and greens and blues and yellows. Was it because they did not wish to offend their sighted neighbors with a display of mismatched clothing and so had decided to refrain from using any colors at all? Was it because they did not wish to draw attention to themselves any more than they already had through the constant tapping of their canes? Were they aware how distracting such sounds could be? Sometimes, when unusually large groups of people outside practiced their blindness all at once and walked in circles around his block, it reminded him of rain dripping from leaves in the forest.

On the other hand, he had never heard of an object from the sky falling onto a blind person. So it was possible this ring of the blind around his block protected him as well as them.

It is not uncommon for a ring of mushrooms to appear around a corpse. He read this one day in the library.

Could the bird have been an osprey? Parsifal did not think so. It could have been a white-tailed kite, known for its grace and buoyancy; however, this particular bird did not seem more or less buoyant than any other. It was definitely too high for a harrier, but what about a Cooper's hawk, or even a northern goshawk, known for its habit of chasing its prey along the forest floor

through thickets and amid underbrush? Parsifal doubted it. It could as easily have been a red-shouldered, or
even red-tailed, hawk, even a Swainson's hawk. Could
it have been a magnificent condor, a throwback to
the Ice Age, whose majestic wings once provided the
model for the so-called Thunderbird sketched on the
walls of sandstone caverns by Native Americans and
since then have become a sort of canary in the mine
for the conservation movement? Possibly, though even
following their reintroduction into the wild they were
still rare, and if it *was* a condor, then in order to accom-
modate the effect of distance it would have to be flying
a lot higher than this one appeared to be.

Parsifal had researched this question, but came to
no conclusion.

Sometimes, in his bed at night, Parsifal lies awake listening to the sounds of objects falling from the sky.
Their pitch, varying according to the size and the shape,
seems like the music of long-lost voices—parents and
their children, perhaps—calling to one another across
some unbridgeable distance.

Fenjewla.

Parsifal once knew a librarian who would be intimate only at times when he told her that he had to leave. Until then, she was indifferent, even distracted, busy looking up some reference or other, but the very moment Parsifal mentioned that he had to leave—to drop off or pick up a pen, for example—she leapt to her feet as if she had been given an electric shock. "Wait, you must kiss me first," she said, and then, before he could say another word, she stepped out of her skirt, which was basically the skirt of a librarian, the kind with ruffles, removed her shoes, which were suited to standing for long periods of time, and unhooked the chain attached to her glasses so she wouldn't lose them. Then she would lead him into the rare books room, which had a lock, or the book repair annex, which did not.

In a way it was pleasant to know how to control the desires of a serious woman such as this librarian easily, and he often took advantage of his knowledge, but after a while, when he really did have to go somewhere in a hurry, it became awkward.

More importantly, however, Parsifal was embarrassed to be the keeper of a secret so close to the center of this woman. He was embarrassed to see a woman whom he cared for so deeply become such easy prey to manipulation, even if it was his own.

"You are a monster," she had told Parsifal the first time he said he had to leave.

And when he left her the last time, her blouse at her feet and the chain from her eyeglasses wrapped around one of the buttons of her sweater, she shouted at him, "Go away, you monster."

Sometimes when Parsifal walks through a market and sees the meat wrapped in its tight skin or plastic or stacked naked in the butcher's case, he thinks: *Surely they also wanted to live.*

It is said that some women actually prefer monsters.

Parsifal wonders if Misty might be one of them.

It was this same librarian who once told Parsifal the following story: A man, forced to spend the night in a graveyard, stumbles into an argument between two ghosts, one of whom is fat and the other thin.

"You will be our judge," says the thinner ghost to the man, and so the man becomes the judge of their argument. Finally, after listening to both sides, he decides the matter, whatever it was, in favor of the thin ghost. And that is when the man's troubles begin, because the losing ghost, the fat one, becomes so outraged he bites off the man's arm and eats it then and there.

Whereupon the thin ghost, the one who has won the argument, feels so bad that this is happening to such an unbiased judge that he takes one of his own arms and replaces the man's arm with it.

So it goes the entire night: the fat ghost eats a part of the man and the thin one replaces whatever has been eaten with a part from himself until, at the end, when morning arrives and the man still has two arms and legs, he can't be sure how much of him is still a man, and how much is a ghost.

Or how much of any of us is past, and how much present? How much is memory, and how much action?

Or, Parsifal added to himself, *how much flesh, and how much scar?*

"This is a very old story," the librarian said when she had finished.

Panic: n. *A sudden, overpowering terror. From Greek* panikos: *of Pan (who would arouse terror in lonely places).* This according to *The American Heritage Dictionary*.

In Parsifal's happiest memories, Pearl is holding Fenjewla as she sings to him:

The silence of a falling star
Lights up a purple sky

That's Hank Williams, she would say, and then, more often than not, she would spit, because living in the forest, particularly in spring with all its pollen, aggravated her allergies.

"But I love the forest," she told him. "And I love you, too." Then, using a rag and the pail of water kept near the door, Pearl rinsed the soup from Fenjewla and handed the cup, clean again, back to her son.

A few days after Parsifal left his message on Misty's answering machine, he thought he saw her on the opposite side of a crowd he had joined. The crowd was examining a huge crater in the ground, arguing whether it had been dug for some reason and the dirt carried away during the night or if it was the result of some new enormous falling object. Nobody had the answer, but the crowd numbered in the hundreds. However, because of the size of the hole and the fact that people had completely surrounded the perimeter, Parsifal could not reach Misty to repeat his message in person before she went away.

If he had reached her, he would have said, "I left you a message. Your pen is ready."

Cannot help but praise what?

Another time, Parsifal returns from the market to find the entire block around his house occupied by many more blind people than usual. This time they are practicing tapping their canes, then tucking them beneath their arms and clapping their hands, before returning their canes to normal use. He guesses that this routine might be some new form of echolocation, but has no way of telling if it's successful or not.

and

   as

     I

       wonder

        where

          you

            are

              I'm

                so

The World of the Forest:	**The World of the City:**
trees	cement
brown green	blue gray
no scars	scars
no shoes	shoes
seed pods and berry juice	pens and ink
foxes and bears	dogs and cats
not seen	seen
mother	father
fire	fire
nature	libraries
not many clothes	clothes
raw mushrooms	frozen vegetables
meat	meat

How much of Parsifal is awake, and how much sleeping?

And, come to think of it, why hasn't Parsifal seen a blind woman among all those blind men who for so long have surrounded his modest house?

Lightning.

III

Parsifal cannot be completely certain, but it seems that the sky is darker than it used to be; quite a bit darker than, say, when he thinks about his forest days, although his eyes were sharper back then. A lot sharper, he remembers, especially because of late he's had some difficulty seeing.

Is there anyone he can check this with? Certainly not Pearl. Are records of such things as brightness kept anywhere? Do libraries have this information? Certainly, the blind men would be not so good to ask, but he could begin by bringing this up with Misty, if she ever arrives to collect her pen, which is working quite well. He knows this because sometimes he'll pick it up and write a line or two.

All journeys end in lovers meeting.

"Journeys end in meetings," people say, but are they right? Do we really need to travel to meet with those we love? Parsifal wonders. *The Old Trapper's Guide to Wood-Craft*, a book his father gave to him, said that if a person is lost in the woods, all he needs to do is stay where he is until rescuers arrive. That is all that is necessary, the book said. Whatever you do, the book said, do not move.

On the other hand, there is the lightning.

On the other hand, there's his name. Or namesake.

So it is settled: Parsifal must journey back to the forest, where he will search for the missing cup, although even if Fenjewla is still there, it isn't guaranteed that he will find it, buried as the cup may be beneath leaves, or fallen trees, or even beneath the bodies of animals who crawled into his old house to die, the way they used to do. When he still lived there, Pearl made him take them outside and dig a hole to bury them. He liked digging holes. A lot.

True, Parsifal knows, it is unlikely that his old house, as poorly constructed as it was, will still be standing, because, frankly speaking, it was always pretty flimsy, and in the years since he lived there, with no one to climb up and replace the branches that had blown off the roof during the night, the house would have to be even worse. For that matter, would the forest even be there? Would the whole forest have been cut down to make space for suburbs?

"Regression," Joe would say.

But if the forest *is* still there, then the door might be too, though possibly covered in branches or buried by leaves. And if he can find the door, then the cup might be nearby, still hanging on a branch or crushed beneath the roof. Unless, of course, someone has already found the door and taken it away to use for his own house, maybe in the suburbs. An unlikely scenario at best, however.

Because it was a very heavy door and, really, how far could a person carry a door like that?

And speaking of unlikely, the nib of the Lady Waterman that Misty left with him did not have the rounded tip that ninety-eight percent of pens have. This one had been ground by someone to a left oblique and retipped. Had Misty done it herself, or had the pen been a gift from a former or present boyfriend? The pen was old, so there was no telling when the work had been done. Parsifal resolved to sound Misty out on the subject the next time they talked, but he would have to do it carefully.

He didn't want to "creep her out," as people say.

On the bark of the tree to which their door was tied Conrad had carved three anchors.

"What are those anchors?" Parsifal asked his father one afternoon when the sun was setting and the canopy of leaves above them was a lovely golden green.

"They represent our family: you, your mother, and me," Conrad answered, "and I carved them on this tree next to the door to our house because you and your mother are my twin anchors of life, along with me, who makes the third."

"Which one am I?" Parsifal asked, and Conrad pointed to the smallest of the three.

An hour later Conrad left to return to the city, and Parsifal never got the chance to ask him how a person could anchor his own life.

Too bad, he thought.

"Excuse me," Parsifal said to one of the blind men who had fallen behind the rest of the blind men who were walking ahead of him in a kind of knot, something that frequently happened, he had noticed, when people "bunched up" because they could not see.

"Excuse me," he repeated.

So the man, who was better dressed than the others, stopped walking and tapping, and turned to face in the direction of the voice that was speaking to him.

"Do you happen to know if there is a forest somewhere in the vicinity?" Parsifal asked.

This man wore a sort of brownish tweed sport coat and a light blue ascot. He pointed his finger into the air as a signal that he wished a moment or two to consider Parsifal's question. Then he moved his head from side to side, squinted, and rubbed his narrow cane against the shin of his left leg. Parsifal noticed that his trousers were unusually well creased, and that his cane, like the canes of all the blind, was white. At last, the man aimed the tip of his cane toward the ground.

"Certainly," the blind man said, "it's not that far from where we are at this very moment. All you need to do is to follow that road"—here he uncannily pointed to one of the several roads leading to and from Parsifal's neighborhood—"until you come to a factory that makes pencils, turn left, and continue for about a mile. I don't see how you can miss it; it's quite well kept, in its way."

Parsifal wanted to ask the man how he and his fellows had chosen his neighborhood to practice their walking. How did they arrive? Were they bussed in or did they walk to get there? Did they sleep together in a dormitory somewhere or inside people's houses? Did they dream, and if so, of what? Instead, he thanked the man, who nodded and continued his moving and tapping away from Parsifal.

Parsifal reentered his house and, using his favorite fountain pen, a classic Parker 51, wrote down the man's instructions so as not to forget them.

"The sand," he had told Joe.

Even though, according to the blind man's directions, the forest was nearby, there was no telling how long it would take him to find his former home—if indeed he could recognize it at all. So Parsifal took out a canteen and filled it with water. He found the travel fountain pen he liked to bring along on trips, a few sheets of decent paper just in case he should be forced to leave a note somewhere, and made five sandwiches—one ham and cheese, two vegetarian-avocado, one turkey-Swiss, and one peanut butter and banana. Also, he packed a hat, a plastic bottle of sunscreen, a fold-up poncho in case of rain, a toothbrush, and a small tube of toothpaste. If nothing else, his years in the forest had taught him the hard way the importance of proper dental hygiene. To all of this he added a box of matches in case he needed to start a fire, an extra pair of socks, and, last but not least, a round compass with a folding top just in case the blind man's directions should prove inaccurate.

By the time Parsifal had assembled everything, it was too late to set off, and so, after eating one of the vegetarian-avocado sandwiches as an early supper, he transferred the remaining ones to the refrigerator and brushed his teeth. Then he lay in bed wondering if those packages of pork or beef or lamb he sometimes passed in meat departments had friends during their brief life spans. Were there familiar faces they were glad to see, or others, now possibly meat themselves, whose days would oft be brightened by their appearance? He remembered that the squirrel that was later eaten by the bear used to follow him around those hours Parsifal released it from its cage, and sometimes birds had dropped down and called to him. Who had Parsifal been to them that they should be so glad to see him? Did those packages of meat in the meat department also feel love, or something close to it? Did they believe their lives had meaning? Did they enjoy spending time "just hanging out" with their friends? Did they like being alone, and if so, what did they think about during those times?

And when they slept their final sleep on beds of Styrofoam, did they dream?

His infinite wisdom.

The following day was sunny and bright, the air crisp and invigorating—a good sign. Parsifal walked and the scenery flew by. He passed an old guy watering his lawn, and an old woman sweeping her sidewalk, and a three-legged dog. The old woman jumped a little when she saw his face, but the old guy and the dog did not. Most miraculous of all, nothing was falling from the sky, at least not near him. True, every so often, far off in the distance, he heard the sound of a falling car radiator, as mournful as a harmonica played around a campfire by a lonesome cowboy, but other than that, the only sounds were birds, insects, and the wind.

Most people, when they first saw his face, became extra friendly, and that's all.

The blind man had been right: in nearly no time Parsifal reached the pencil factory and it was an impressive sight. Surrounded by a yellow wooden fence, the factory yard was as big as a football field, with the factory building itself off to one side, squatting between the two thirty-yard lines. At one end of the yard were piles of trees stacked in squares two stories high, and at the other end were gray cones of powdered graphite, looking like the gigantic teepees of some depressed Indian tribe. Between them, sprawling in the sun, was a miniature city made of pallets loaded with boxes of yellow pencils sealed in clear plastic. Outside the gates, heaps of sawdust waited to be hauled away. Parsifal saw that the factory, like many buildings those days, had reinforced its roof to prevent damage from falling objects.

A turkey-Swiss would taste great, he thought, and found a bus bench across from the pencil plant and sat down.

That was when Parsifal noticed the bird above his head.

"To live is to suffer," a librarian once told Parsifal after they had finished being intimate on her foldout couch. They were watching a documentary about a drought in Africa on the local public television station. Then she added, as an afterthought, "Present company excepted."

Of course, it was also possible that the bird was not a bird at all, but a remote-controlled aircraft, programmed by some anonymous controller back at "the base" to follow Parsifal day in and day out. But how then would it refuel? There would have to be at least two craft, and one would replace the other when the first had run out of gas, or whatever kind of fuel it used. True, he had never seen the two of them together, but he hadn't been watching the sky at all times, and they could have traded places under cover of the dark.

Also, there was the question (if it *was* an aircraft and not a bird) of how it knew it was *him*. The first possibility was that a camera, possibly infrared, might be on board, and the images transmitted of him going about his daily business would appear on a screen in a room somewhere, in front of a technician trained to monitor such reception. (Parsifal imagined a screen with crosshairs to keep him centered.) It would be the technician's job to move the aircraft as Parsifal moved. Perhaps a skilled technician could even keep track of two or three such aircraft—that is, assuming there were more people than him being tracked.

A second and more cost-effective explanation was that at one point or another he personally had been outfitted with some sort of homing device, a small metal transmitter that told the drone, or whatever it was, where to find him, where to train its mechanical eye. But how would such a homing device have been attached? When he thought about it, it could have been at almost any time: Just the other day, for example, Ben, his normally genial barber, had apologized for accidentally striking the top of Parsifal's head with his scissors' point, but had it really been an accident? Or could it have been his dentist, Doctor Spolidoro? Who knew what went on in one's mouth when one's tooth was being filled? Or how about the doctor, whatever his name was, who had performed a colonoscopy a little while back?

Still, once he entered the protective canopy of the forest there was a good chance that whatever it was, whether a bird or a drone, would not find it so easy to follow him.

Well, a pretty good chance.

A fair chance.

Frequently strangers will ask, "Parsifal, are your parents still alive?"

He does not know what compels people to inquire about such things, but he hopes it is sympathy, and not pity. When he tells them they are not, they inevitably add that they are sorry, though why *they* should be sorry is puzzling, because they have never met his parents, and, when Parsifal points this out, the conversation stops and they walk away.

As a result, these people never have a chance to hear how Conrad, his father, who spent a large part of his life hating the forest and mostly remained a stranger to it, disappeared one day never to be seen again. Or how Pearl, who had spent much of her life believing the forest would protect her, came to be disappointed in the end.

First do no harm.

Which brings up, in a way, that whole business with the Happy Bunny Preschool.

Or it may be that a monster is simply anyone who does not ask the question as to whether he is a monster or he isn't.

Parsifal thought that was what he should have told the librarian when she brought the subject up, but by then she had disappeared.

He should have asked Joe, but now he was gone, too.

"It rains in my heart like it rains on the town; so what exactly is this sadness that creeps into my heart?" The Frenchman Paul Verlaine would not be asking that question, Parsifal thought, if he had grown up in the forest, wrapped in an itchy wool blanket, lying on a bed of crumpled stock certificates, listening to the drip, drip, drip of the rain on the leaves (so like the tapping of blind men's canes!), feeling the dark of everything that was the past and the dark of all still to come, secure in the knowledge that any dream in search of a recipient would surely not be able to find its way over the leaf-strewn paths and obscure trails of animals to his home, his bed, his sleeping self.

Nonetheless, when Parsifal thought of that beautiful sadness of his past, which was so unlike the anxious, somewhat panicky sadness of his present, how he longed to feel it once again.

Fenjewla.

He finished his sandwich. It was the turkey-Swiss.

Materials most commonly used for the bodies of pens are resin, acrylic, hard rubber, silver, wood, celluloid, and sometimes, more unusually, gold, abalone, mother of pearl, even deer horn or leather (this latter not a body exactly, but stretched tight to cover the inexpensive plastic core lying beneath it).

Sometimes I take a great notion
*   To jump in the river and drown*

Conrad sang that.

And "Goodnight, Irene" was right.

A mile later, he came to a florist.
   Forest. Florist.
   That stupid blind man, Parsifal thought, *must have had wax in his ears*. And despite the popular mythology regarding sensory compensation that comes with blindness, at least in this case the removal of one sense had not strengthened the others.

Parsifal entered the florist shop, just because he was already there.

For some reason, though he had not traveled so very far that day, he had begun to limp. Falling down as often as he had back in the forest, his ankles were fairly weak, though it was hard to say if they had been weak to begin with or if it was a result of all that falling.

The florist shop seemed more a haphazard collection of plants that had grown up on their own (but in pots) and in no particular order than an actual enterprise. Daisies were with orchids; ferns shared their space with cacti, roses, and lilies; chrysanthemums with irises and carnations; all swept up in the same net, like members of some far-flung criminal conspiracy.

"Your face," the smock-wearing woman behind the counter said as Parsifal walked in.

"I'm sorry," he said, and was about to explain, but she produced a wet cloth from somewhere and handed it to him.

"It's red. It looks as if you've been out in the sun."

He took the cloth and laid it across his face. The cloth was cool, and smelled faintly of lemons.

She was a normal-looking person, with the plump, friendly countenance that might have been on a bottle of syrup or a box of cake mix, except that she was wearing glasses. "Thanks," Parsifal said and then, realizing it would have been rude for him to simply turn around and leave, he looked for something to buy to show his gratitude.

"How much are those?" he asked, pointing to a bucket of red tulips at the side of the counter.

"Twelve for ten dollars," she said.

"I'll take six," he told her. So the woman wrapped them in cellophane and added a stalk of ferns and a white ribbon. They looked nice.

"Thanks," Parsifal said, and left. *Maybe I'll give them to Misty.*

Rains in my _____ like it rains on the _____.

Halfway back to his house, Parsifal saw a small red drink cooler fall about sixty feet away and bounce off a mailbox. He walked over to it. The cooler was empty, as he thought it would be, but when he looked up into the sky from where it had fallen, he noticed that the bird, or whatever it was that had been following him, seemed to have added downward swoops to its pattern of circles, as if it were trying to get closer.

The mailbox was completely undamaged.

On the other hand, perhaps Parsifal should not blame the blind man. A librarian once told him that he needed to work on his enunciation.

What Parsifal remembered of his leaving the forest was this: Walking away from trees, a few leaves still stuck in his hair, a few scratches still leaking blood, limping a little, barefoot, the trees becoming smaller, and then, before he reached the city—maybe halfway between the city and the forest, so that the trees were no longer even visible—a woman walking toward him. She was wearing a pink dress and hiking sandals. Her blond hair was pulled back into a neat ponytail, and when she saw him she made a small, startled sound.

So as not to further upset her, he crossed to the other side of the road, which was, at that point, a two-lane highway.

In his memory, this woman resembles Misty, but it could not have been Misty, because at that time Misty would have been no more than a child.

The low-grade nausea that creeps into his heart.

Parsifal wondered if the trails he remembered from the forest were still there or if they had become overgrown. At the exact moment he wondered this, he looked down and noticed he was no longer carrying any flowers.

I must have left them somewhere.

When Parsifal returned home from the florist, he made his way to his front door through the circle of the blind men that surrounded his house. That day, however, their numbers had thinned, so there was not even a circle, but more like two or three very slow electrons orbiting around a nucleus. His house looked the same as it had when he left. It was what people call "a cottage," though he was unsure what they mean by that. It was covered with gray wood siding and had a front porch he never used. The front door opened and shut easily. When he thought about it, it seemed a little tame after all his time in the forest.

Sand.

Once inside, he ate the leftover sandwiches and fell asleep.

Parsifal woke to a radio bulletin that an entire town north of where he lived had been destroyed by a bombardment of two-wheeled vehicles: motorcycles, mopeds, and bicycles. True, it was not a large town, but this was the first time he knew of that such a large-scale sky-related, concentrated disaster had occurred. Over one hundred people had been killed, the media excitedly reported, forgetting to mention the usual famines, earthquakes, and floods killing thousands.

Never had the sky felt more dangerous to him.

The next day brought a report of a large brushfire in the middle of the state, one that filled the sky with soot for nearly one hundred square miles. The fire had been started by a group of hikers who were burned to death.

His infinite wisdom.

IV

f the source of one's pain comes from an ill-considered action, does that make the pain any less? If a person hurts his ankle, say, by seeing how many times he can hop on one foot in his kitchen, and then maybe lets his attention wander for a minute to a line of blind men outside his window, so he winds up taking a bad hop and hits his head on the corner of a cabinet, is the pain any less? Parsifal wonders about this.

Or does it hurt more?

According to the map Parsifal picked up the following day at a map store, the forest he wanted to visit was actually not very near his home at all, but about a hundred miles north and to the east of the city. The fact that he had forgotten how far away it was he can only attribute to the clouded state of mind he must have possessed when he first left the forest, a state of mind that compressed the memory of several days of travel, limping and hungry, into only a few hours.

Could he be wrong about other details of his past as well?

Parsifal thought the woman who sold him the map at the store was similar to the woman at the florist shop, the one who patted his hand as she handed him the tulips he had bought. However, while the woman at the florist shop was dressed in a light blue smock and a flowered blouse, the woman at the map store was dressed in a plain brown suit that had epaulettes on the shoulders and many pockets, as if she were preparing to leave at any minute on a journey, making ready to fill each of those pockets with maps. Both women wore glasses.

A collapsible hiking pole leaned against the store's front counter. The woman's hair was in a bun. Her muscles were firm and her skin was tan. She was not the sort of person whose face might be chosen for a box of cake mix, but possibly for a granola blend with oatmeal, almonds, and cranberries.

"That's right," she told Parsifal when he'd asked if she had ever been there. "It's not a short walk to the forest from here, but I think you'll like it."

He told her that he had lived there for a while.

"Well then," she replied, "I'll bet that you have a whole lot of fond memories."

Somewhere there must be a word, some technical term, for a combination of anticipation, nostalgia, and dread.

When he thinks about fountain pens, Parsifal often thinks about ink windows—those clear sections of the body of a pen that enable a user to see how much ink remains. Not all pens have them—most do not—but of those that do, there are basically three types (other than those "demonstrator" pens, which are clear plastic in order to demonstrate the pen's working mechanism). The first kind of window is a thin, transparent ring about an inch away from the base of the nib. It's efficient and easy to use. The second is a transparent stripe, or several stripes, running along the barrel of the pen that alternates clear with colored strips. The third has transparent spots scattered about the length of the pen. With all three, a person can hold the pen up to a light and instantly tell how much ink remains. The disadvantage of an ink window is that it interrupts the design, most noticeably with the ring-type window, unless, of course, you consider the ring a part of the pattern. The advantage of ink windows is that a person knows when he is going to run out of ink, so before embarking on any extended sequence of thoughts he does not wish to have interrupted by jumping up and taking a trip to "Mister Bottle," he can fill his pen before he starts. Knowing when the ink will run out seems a little like knowing the date of your death. Some people want that information. Others, like Parsifal, would prefer to be surprised.

Homecoming.

In the forest, Parsifal and Pearl played a kind of game. His mother would send him out of their little house, ordering him to leave a trail of pebbles or small, hard pieces of bread—whichever Pearl happened to have handy—so that he might find his way back. "Walk somewhere for several hours," she would tell him, "but don't forget to leave behind some markers so you can find your way home again."

When at last Parsifal would return (although sometimes it would take a day or two) she would hug him and laugh. "*Mein kleiner Hansel*," she would say, rubbing her fingers through his hair.

Hansel?

The loneliness of being alone.

And did Pearl ever learn that Parsifal sometimes tricked her? That instead of making a trail, he had only walked to the nearest hollow tree, a few yards away, and then curled up and slept inside of it for six or seven hours?

Now it's too late to ask.

If pressed on the subject of the cup, Parsifal will admit that he could have taken Fenjewla with him, but—he never fails to add—because he was in the midst of a crisis situation, he considers having left the cup behind forgivable.

"It happened like this," Parsifal explained during one of his therapy sessions with Joe. "I had gone out one afternoon in search of food, because my father, Conrad, was delayed from arriving with supplies. This was not uncommon, nor was it unusual that I found myself too far away to walk back home again by nightfall. It was always dangerous to walk in the forest at night, so I built a small campfire, and then, in the morning, left it safely confined within its ring of stones to burn out by itself, because—and here is the single place where I differ with the book on woodcraft my father left with me—if you are properly trained in woodcraft and are certain the fire is unable to spread, there is absolutely no danger in leaving it that way. Also, if a person needs to return quickly to his campsite, he can find it fast by following the wisp of smoke."

"Then," Parsifal continued, "I hurried home, and it was a good thing I did, because by the time I arrived my mother was waiting.

"'You know,' Pearl said, 'with my heightened sense of smell, I believe I can smell a fire. It's far away right now, but I think it's coming closer, and a person can't be too careful firewise. Maybe this is exactly the right time for you to take a trip to the city and see if you can track down your father. I'll stay here and take care of things. Don't worry about me. You go. I'll be all right.'"

A condition of Parsifal's release from jail by the court was that he make regular visits to Joe.

What is the sound of sadness creeping into his heart?

And Pearl was right: the fire, from wherever it began, had moved quickly. Within half an hour it was nearly at their house. "There was only time enough to throw a few items into a burlap sack," Parsifal said to Joe, "and not time enough to look around for every little thing I might want to take, such as my foolish metal cup named Fenjewla."

"My mother," he added, "was wearing her ordinary outfit: a leather apron attached at her sides by strings of animal sinew. Around her shoulders was a stole made out of a couple of fox skins she had sewn together, and beneath that, a fancy black lace bra that Conrad had brought her from the city. As usual," he said, "my mother wore no shoes or socks. (The soles of her feet were incredibly tough, and she would frequently challenge me to try to pierce them with a sharp stick, but I never succeeded.) On her head was the kind of hat she liked to wear, fashioned out of an abandoned bird's nest—'Just for fun,' she used to say."

Pearl insisted on accompanying him to the edge of the forest even though Parsifal had said there was no need. "Don't you worry," she said. "I know this forest well, and the fire will never get here. It's just that you are long overdue to leave, and as hard as it is for me to imagine a life here without fixing your scrapes and bruises, and mending your clothes, too—today, with this fire, is as good a day as any for you to start your journey."

"And, Joe," Parsifal said, "I was just about to kiss her good-bye, but that moment she coughed and picked up a damp handkerchief to hold against her face, so in the end I just walked down the road, thinking I would come back again and tell her all about my adventures.

"'Have a good life in the city,' she told me. 'And if you see your father, Conrad, give him my best. *Au revoir*. That's French for *so long*,' my mother added."

Au revoir, Parsifal said he called back, his last sight of her standing with her foot on a stump at the forest's edge, the air smoky with good-byes. *Au revoir*.

"Fenjewla?" Joe said, looking confused.

On some days Parsifal seems to exist even to himself as only a soundtrack: there is no person to be seen, just the sounds of his footsteps crossing the floor, the sounds of water running, stopping, more footsteps, the sounds of a door creaking open, then swinging shut, the sigh of a cushion being sat on. How much better this is, he thinks, than the constant oppression of sight, the con-

stant bracketing of his life by everything around him:
vases, tables, trees, the mirrors in barber shops. On such
days there are only sounds and Parsifal—equals in their
invisibility. Thinking of this, for the first time he begins to envy those familiar cane-tapping, hard-walking,
blind individuals.

Not that Parsifal ever thought less of Joe for having
been appointed by the courts.

His second attempt to set out for the forest took more
preparation than the first, which, after all, did not go
so very far. Instead of five sandwiches Parsifal took six-
teen, a candle, matches, a sleeping bag, and four pairs of
socks. He carried a canteen full of water, a pocket comb,
a pocketknife, and, of course, the map he had purchased
from the map store. His plan was this: First he would
walk to the bus station, where he would buy a ticket for
a bus that would take him to the forest. Next he would
spend one night (maybe two) in the forest searching for
the cup and then, if he hadn't found it, return by bus.

Parsifal checked his house to make certain that he
had not left any water running or pots on the stove.
Then he walked outside and in the direction of the bus
station, noticing in the process that the circle of the

blind had filled with new walkers. A few of the blind people parted to let him through and then, after he had passed, the circle closed again.

Were the blind growing in numbers? It seemed as though they might be.

Above his head, the bird was circling. Or making spirals.

"*Au revoir*," Parsifal told the blind men.

To see you again.

Parsifal was about halfway to the bus station when he heard the distinctive whir of a new kind of bomb that, he had read, the sky was using: dozens of ball bearings taken out of the crankshafts of vehicles and then released all at once, blanketing an area. According to the reports, this would soon be followed by the pieces of the actual crankshaft. It was deadly, of course, but the commentary regarding the choice of weapons was divided. Some believed it represented an advance on the part of the sky, while others were of the opinion it was a sign that whoever was in charge of this was running out of things to drop. He couldn't be sure if the sound of the descending bearings was more like a waterfall, a fountain, or a single strum of a harp, and knew that although it should have been easy to tell one from the other, for some reason it wasn't.

The silence of a falling star

When Parsifal reached the bus station he could no longer see the bird.

Back in the forest, Parsifal took a little time every day to imagine Conrad, his father, working at his office in the city. In Parsifal's mind, Conrad sits, wearing his dark, pin-striped suit of fine wool, in his stuffed leather desk chair with wheels and an adjustable back. Meanwhile, as the manicured fingers of one of his father's hands flip through a stack of stock prospectuses, the other holds a phone to his ear, listening to a client. Behind Conrad stands his secretary, whose name, Parsifal knows, is Margot, and she is dressed in a light blue business suit. True, the skirt is possibly cut too short to technically qualify as proper business attire, but still— according to his father—it's well within the limits of good taste. Meanwhile, Margot massages his father's shoulders, then pauses to reach forward slightly over him, her breast just brushing his father's arm as she brings a steaming cup of cappuccino to Conrad's lips, which are dry from so much listening. The coffee cup is filled to the very top with whipped cream.

Near Conrad, on the floor, kneels Jimmy, the traveling shoeshine boy who carries his homemade box stuffed full of rags and polish from office to office all day long. The boy is forced to use the stairs—his father once reported to Parsifal, Conrad's voice rising with indignation—because to see him on the elevator, his sneakers falling apart, his hair poking out beneath his filthy cap, offends the so-called "better-class" folks who need to ride the elevator up and down to their offices each day.

"A disgraceful situation," Conrad told his son, "but you must understand that the ways of capitalism can be cruel at times." Conrad also told Parsifal that Jimmy coughed frequently because he suffered from a chronic lung disorder.

Meanwhile, *cough, cough.*

"What's that noise?" Parsifal's father's client asks him on his end of the phone.

"Oh that," Conrad answers. "I was just moving some furniture around."

And so, Jimmy, his fingers dark with polish, caresses Parsifal's father's shoes, a happy smile on his lips, because, having to support not only himself but also his mother and his crippled sister, he is glad to be working for a client as generous as the one before him at that moment, by whom he means Parsifal's father. Margot looks down at the young boy and smiles.

"If only you could be as self-sufficient as young Jimmy," Conrad used to admonish Parsifal, and then he would follow this wish with some new, heartbreaking detail from the shoeshine boy's life for Parsifal to mull over.

The bus station was packed as usual. It had been that way ever since air traffic had been suspended due to the attacks, or whatever they were, from the sky. All around Parsifal people were weeping, laughing, greeting friends and family, or just standing dazed from having to get up and walk around after sitting for so many hours. Some buses, of course, had cramped restrooms in the rear, but generally they were too filled with cigarette smokers or irritable bowel sufferers to allow anyone else much access. Around Parsifal, brawny drivers strode about in smart gray uniforms, carrying overnight bags and wearing mock military caps with badges of ringed golden tires on their peaks. Many were former airline pilots put out of business by the general idleness of airplanes.

Also, there were vendors selling from colorful carts, magazine stands, and stands where people could buy tapes with inspirational messages, as well as places to download music, for a fee, into their music players. Mingling unobtrusively with the crowd were plain-clothes cops on the alert for pickpockets, bunko artists, and sellers of forged bus tickets that could be purchased for a fraction of the price of a real one and worked just as well. Parsifal approached one of these fake-ticket sellers, a nicely dressed gentleman wearing a bright green vest who was leaning on a coffee machine and had indicated he might have a few tickets available by means of first rubbing his fingers together and then putting his hands into his armpits and discreetly raising and lowering his elbows.

Just to be sure, Parsifal asked, "Do you have any tickets to the forest?"

The man named a price.

"I'll take one."

"Hey pal, you've got yourself a real bargain."

"Thanks."

When he first arrived in the city, Parsifal was assigned a public health social worker. She had him take a bath, bought him a new set of clothing made of denim, burned his old clothes, and found him a room at the YMCA. She then enrolled him in the local high school and gave him enough money to live on. When he graduated from high school, which didn't take long because of the excellent training his parents had given him, it was up to him to find a new place to stay and a job.

The sadness that seeps into my heart.

Sometimes Parsifal wondered how his parents ever met.

"It was at a dance," his mother once told him, and when he pressed her for details she claimed not to remember. "The only thing I could think about the whole time I was there was your father," Pearl said.

But what kind of dance could it have been in the middle of the forest?

One afternoon, waiting for a librarian to get off work, Parsifal read about mountain climbing. The book stated that at times a climber can go thirty or forty feet straight up without a problem, and then the climber will hit a ledge that may take half a day to get around.

The book said that climbers climbed because it was there.

"It" being the mountain.

That same afternoon, he found a book about fountain pens. It was then, undistracted by the snores and snuffles of others using the library, that he rekindled his interest in fountain pens, which had begun so many years ago in the forest but until that moment had lain dormant.

The bus driver turned out to be one of the very same men Parsifal had witnessed earlier carrying an overnight bag and striding confidently across the bus terminal. His name, according to the rectangular plastic label made to look like metal on the front of his gray uniform, was Nick. He told Parsifal to take a seat. Then he returned to looking at something on a clipboard and began to rev the engine. His hair was brown and starting to thin.

When the rest of the passengers had arrived and been seated, Nick turned off the bus's interior lights and told everyone to make themselves comfortable. Then he released the hand brake, and the bus slowly rolled out of the station almost directly into a red light, where it had to wait a while longer. Nick used his time to give the engine some additional revs but, all in all, appeared annoyed, and this delay, as slight as it was, seemed an ill omen to Parsifal as well, though riding as he was on a forged ticket, he didn't feel he could complain.

And it had been that same public health social worker who had come to his school and called him out of class to tell him the tragic story of his mother. It seemed that Pearl, minutes after waving good-bye to him, crazed and disoriented by a mixture of panic over the fire's spread and probably feeling grief over the loss of her only son, as well—much as any animal caught in a fire's path—had apparently taken at least one wrong turn, had become engulfed in flames, herself, and had burst into the backyard of a family that was holding—as if in defiance of the conflagration all around them—a barbeque of their own. And though they attempted to douse her with a hose, the water came sadly much too late. It had taken weeks for the authorities to find him and tell him the news, his social worker, whose name was Mrs. Knightly, said.

It was already late by the time the bus left the station— well past dusk. This meant that Parsifal would be arriving at the forest in the middle of the night, something he had not thought about earlier.

Hansel, indeed.

Is it surprising that a person raised in the forest would be wary of strangers?

Not at all. In Parsifal's case, most of the strangers he encountered there had been hunters who, strictly speaking, did not have human interaction as their goal, but instead were prone to taking pot shots at him when they spotted him in one part of the forest or another. It wasn't so much that he resembled a deer—Parsifal knew that—but after a hunter had spent an entire day carrying around his heavy firearm or sitting strapped to some tree, Parsifal could understand how a person would be happy just to have something to shoot at.

Actually, many of them wound up shooting trees as well, and though Parsifal understood "where they were coming from" (a phrase he later learned that described a whole range of aberrant human behavior), such understanding made him less, not more, trusting of people.

Parsifal had never seen a woman hunter.

To be seen or be unseen? To be seen is to endure the acidic gaze of others. To be unseen, to be in the dark, is like having bandages soaked in wet baking soda applied where a person has been burned by something or other as yet uncataloged, but possibly acidic in nature.

And yet, in being seen, one's existence is somehow confirmed, while being invisible . . . well, you know . . .

The inside of the bus was dark. Parsifal's seatmate, who had already gotten the place by the window, was an old man, roughly the age Conrad would be if he were still alive, but unlike his father, this man had a huge head, short prickly red hair, a rough stubbly beard, pocked skin, and large inflamed knuckles. After a couple of hours, the stranger turned toward Parsifal and stuck out a hand.

"Where are you headed?" the man asked.

"Only as far as the forest," was Parsifal's reply.

The man appeared to give this some thought; then the bus stopped.

Parsifal picked up his backpack and stepped out into the dark, relieved to have come to the end of this particular conversation.

One day, on the occasion of Parsifal's ninth birthday, when Conrad had come up from the city to celebrate, at the beginning of the meal Pearl announced that she would no longer eat any recognizable part of an animal. "Touching their little legs makes me too sad," she told her husband and her son. "You eat them yourselves."

So after that, Parsifal (and Conrad on those few occasions he was around) would be left with a plate of legs, arms, ribs, necks, and even ears, while Pearl ate whatever shapeless and anonymous organ happened to be in front of her at the time. "Don't tell me what this is from," she would say. "It would only upset me."

Then, almost as a premonition of their final separation, the day before the forest fire, Pearl changed her dietary restrictions. "It was a phase," she told Parsifal, snatching a juicy joint from his plate, "and like all phases it had its uses, but now it's over and your mother is ready to move on."

What is this sadness that slithers into my heart?

Parsifal watched the bus pull away. There was no moon, and the red dots of the bus's taillights grew small until he could follow them no longer. The night air was getting cold, so he reached into his backpack and pulled out the insulated jacket he'd thought to pack. Parsifal looked at his hands and could barely see them.

It was very, very dark.

Overhead Parsifal heard the cries of owls, and behind them the distant whoosh of wind through branches. Old memories came back: branches falling on his head, twisting his ankle on a log that suddenly slipped to one side, the smell of smoke. Far away from the road was a spot of yellow light, and above it, he could barely make out a sign, Motel de la Forêt. *Motel of the Forest*, he thought to himself.

Parsifal shouldered his backpack and began to walk toward the sign.

The sadness that walks into my heart.

The dark felt good on Parsifal's face. Suddenly, about thirty feet to his left, he heard a thump. He walked over and saw a fresh scar driven into the earth by what looked to be—it was hard to tell without a moon—a deep-fat turkey fryer. Night attacks were nothing new; for one thing, as long as there was no particular target other than the earth itself, no aiming was required. Still, Parsifal couldn't remember having heard of turkey fryers ever being used as weapons. Until then, he couldn't remember them ever being used for anything at all but frying turkeys.

Races into my heart.

Sometimes, after Parsifal first arrived in the city, he used to see, in the midst of a crowd, an immaculately groomed man at a distance. More often than not, the man walking away from him would be wearing a dark pin-striped suit, and Parsifal would imagine that the man was his father. So he would pick up his pace, nearly running, until he pulled alongside the stranger and he could stare fully into his face.

It was never Conrad.

When people try to recall the exact time that things started to fall from the sky, the answer is always vague. Certainly there was a long history of things dropping, but at the beginning those incidents were relatively few and widely spaced. Then people noticed that sort of thing was happening more often, until one day, after the dedication of an eighteen-hole golf course was interrupted by a few dozen brand-new batteries taking out two caddies and a pro, public attention grew. Not that anyone could do anything about it, of course, but for a time each and every event, no matter how small, was covered nightly on the evening news. Now, however, events such as these are so commonplace that it takes an unusual occurrence to capture the public's attention.

Parsifal's crest: three white anchors on a field of green samite.

Samite: *A heavy silk fabric, often interwoven with gold or silver, worn in the Middle Ages.*

Middle English *samit*, from Old French, from Medieval Latin *examitum*, from Medieval Greek *hexamiton*, from Greek, neuter of *hexamitos*, of six threads: *hexa-*, hexa- + *mito*s, warp thread. That's what the *American Heritage Dictionary* has to say.

"And whose heritage would that be, anyway?" Joe wanted to know.

V

n the winter in the forest, Parsifal would wake with a thin layer of ice on his eyelids, so that before he could open them he would have to tap each one lightly with the forefinger of his right hand to shatter the frozen film. Thinking about it now, the tap and then the release that followed was like nothing he has felt since—a way to start each day that resembled walking out of a prison into the world. At least, that is how it felt to him, after he had left the forest and finished his high school education but before he had met his first librarian, walking out of prison, a free man, albeit with several strings attached, one of them being court-mandated visits to a therapist.

"Regressive," Joe would have said.

The Motel de la Forêt was a low building with six units and no swimming pool. In front of each unit, though difficult to make out in the dark, was a small, smudged barbecue grill. Off to one side there was a large tent, the purpose of which was a mystery. In front of the motel's office, Parsifal wiped his feet on a mat made of bottle caps and pushed the bell. It was late; he hoped someone would answer and not be frightened by his arriving in the middle of the night. The sign by the road had read "VACANCY."

Finally a light went on and the door opened—cautiously, Parsifal thought—onto an office area of knotty pine, cuckoo clocks, and a counter on which rested three statues of squirrels made from acorns glued together. In front of one of them was a small sign that read "For Sale," though no price was given.

The woman who stood before him wore a heavy red robe with gold threads running through it, backless slippers, and a sort of turban, the kind some women don after washing their hair. In a way, she resembled the woman at the florist shop, and also the woman at the map store, in her calm demeanor and the fact that she wore glasses, but in most other ways she did not.

"I'm looking for a room," Parsifal said. "It's just for one night. I hadn't planned to have to stay in a motel, actually, but I'm afraid I got here later than I'd expected."

"That will be thirty bucks," the woman told him.

When Parsifal had trouble falling asleep, he thought about the trees in the forest, large and small, smooth barked and rough, how all of them were there waiting in the dark—upright, parallel, and patient. They were confident that the sun would be out the next day, those trees were. The night will pass, the trees seemed to say. *All we have to do is to wait.*

Fragments, true enough.

The trees were fragments, too.

His room at the Motel de la Forêt continued the same knotty-pine motif as the motel's office. There was a fake Indian bedspread, a fake pine dresser, and a fake Indian rug on the floor. They were miles from Indians, as far as Parsifal knew, but possibly the owner of the motel, or the decorator, was unaware of that fact. More authentically, there was the head of a deer on the wall, but it was turned slightly so its aggrieved eyes watched him as he sat on the bed. A framed photograph, evidently taken some time ago, judging by the clothes of the people in it, hung on the wall facing the foot of the bed. It showed a man, a woman, and a child. Evidently it had been snowing, and the three were gathered before an open hole no more than eighteen inches from side to side. There were three sets of footprints leading up to it, but how the hole had come to be there was a mystery. Was it a grave for a beloved pet, or was that hole one of the first—perhaps the very first—salvo in the sky's attack on the earth that has continued to this day?

The backs of the three were toward the camera, and there was little else to see except that the child held in his right hand some small object, possibly a toy, or a book, or, for that matter, it could even be a cup.

"What have you done?" the deer's head on the wall seemed to be saying.

The logo of the Pelikan pen is of a mother pelican feeding her young, but that bird circling overhead was certainly no pelican.

In the middle of the night Parsifal was awakened from a dreamless sleep by a knocking on the door of his room.

"Just a minute," he called out, and as quickly as he could he found his pants, shoes, shirt, and socks to put them on, but by the time he opened the door, no one was there at all.

"Hello," he called out into the night.

His voice echoed in the trees and no one answered.

The sound of a person shouting into a grave.

The deer. Silence.

One other pen-filling system is the sleeve, or vacuum filler, which is a variation of the eyedropper in which the ink is sucked up a hollow tube like a straw. Capillary fillers and various sorts of button fillers are really just variants of the rubber ink sac.

While in the forest, Parsifal and Pearl mostly lived on things like mushrooms, pine nuts, certain ferns, and— the occasional animal part aside—especially on the dried beans Conrad brought with him on his visits. On the nights Conrad visited, Parsifal was first alerted to his father's presence by a chorus of snapping twigs and muttered curses, until finally he would see his father's middle-sized frame carrying a fifty-pound sack of beans (or sometimes brown rice or millet), along with all the various other things he had put into cloth bags and attached to his belt, staggering through the trees toward their house.

The only time Parsifal slept with a woman who was not a librarian he found himself missing their ways: the methodical unbuttoning of their clothing, how they took care to fold each piece after they removed it and placed it carefully on a nearby shelf or chair where they could find it again quickly, their patience as they waited for him to finish whatever he was doing before they asked a question or delivered a piece of helpful information, and the way they never, ever seemed surprised by his appearance. In contrast, the non-librarian threw her clothing everywhere and was full of opinions, which she was only too happy to share. She told him he looked "interesting."

"Sand," he had answered Joe's question.

The continental breakfast buffet at the Motel de la Forêt was served outdoors in the extralarge tent he had seen the night before. For Parsifal, eating in public had never been an enjoyable experience. Being so exposed immediately upon waking seemed cruel indeed, but in this case, his fellow breakfasters were hardly offensive. They consisted of an old Danish-speaking couple, a family of four (a mother, father, and a set of overweight twins), plus a blind person whose guide dog, a yellow Lab, looked reproachfully at the rest of the breakfasters, as it if were their fault his master could not see.

No, there was nothing monstrous about this crowd. True, the twins' mother had scooped up all the pats of genuine butter and stuck them in her purse before anyone else had the chance to take one; the blind man stuck his finger in each pot of jam to test the flavor; and the old Danes began their meal by clearing their throats and depositing whatever they had found objectionable in them in the grass at the base of their chairs; but within minutes they all were refilling each other's coffees and slapping each other's backs as if they'd been friends for years. Even the twins had gone outside the tent to play with the Labrador, who, understanding his master was in good hands, had decided it could relax.

So what had they ever done to Parsifal?

Sometimes Parsifal liked to listen to the sounds of old performances of music that had been recorded in front of audiences.

The dead applauding the dead.

Whether or not that circling, or spiraling, bird or
drone—whichever it was—was still above Parsifal after he had finished the breakfast he couldn't tell. The
morning mist was especially heavy, and it was impossible to see much higher than the tops of the surrounding trees. Parsifal poured himself two cups of coffee,
ate a slice of melon and two pieces of dry toast with
raspberry jam. Then he walked outside the tent to eat a
third piece of toast, this one with a drizzle of honey. In
the daylight the motel looked even more rustic, if that
was possible. The tent was striped in green and white.
Strewn around the lawn were statues of squirrels and
raccoons and tiny deer. The other guests were still eating, but it was time for him to leave.

"You have a real love of books," a librarian once told
Parsifal. "I bet it comes from your name."

So Parsifal had just walked back inside the tent to say
good-bye to his fellow guests, when one of the twins
was killed by a falling propane cylinder. At first, all
Parsifal knew was that both children had been playing outside and there was a terrific thud, but when he,
along with everyone else, rushed outside to see what
had happened, they found a hole in the earth with a

bloody hand lying next to it. There was no mistaking that small hand even if they had wanted to. The other twin stood and watched, as the Lab held in his mouth a yellow tennis ball he had found somewhere.

This was the first time Parsifal had personally witnessed the lethal power of an attack from the sky. But as bad as it was (and it *was* bad), he also knew there was nothing he, or anyone else, could do, so after several minutes had passed he took advantage of the confusion among the other guests to slip away unnoticed.

On those days when Pearl was feeling optimistic, she would add to the end of every sentence: "But don't worry, one day things will change."

"Why couldn't it have been the blind guy?" Parsifal heard the twins' mother ask.

One afternoon as he was squatting by the stream in the forest, watching tadpoles growing their legs and shrinking their tails, et cetera, his mother called him. "Parsifal," she said, "I'm afraid I have some bad news for you. I have a terrible feeling your father has just killed himself in remorse over a collapsed financial transaction, one in which his investors lost millions. Don't ask me how I know," Pearl said. "I just do."

But then a couple of weeks later Conrad returned, his back bent nearly double under a sack of lentils this time, his briefcase, containing a new supply of defunct bond certificates, tied to his belt.

Groups gather around a corpse.

Parsifal used to fear that in one of the earth's great counterattacks on the sky his forest might be set on fire again, that those trees he had loved and grown up with, the animals, too—the deer, and squirrels, and raccoons, and field mice, and opossums, and foxes—would be turned to smoke and ash for no other reason than spite: to choke the sky with their reconstituted bodies. But now that he was there, at the edge of his forest, looking at it in daylight, for no good reason at all Parsifal felt confident that this would never happen.

But then, Parsifal had never thought his mother would die in a forest fire.

It was an interesting experience to be seated across from the blind man at the continental breakfast and to be able to peer so deeply into his eyes, whose irises reminded him of the bottoms of mushrooms—those little flutes, or gills, or whatever they are called.

The silence of a falling star
Lights up a purple sky

Pearl sang that.

Frequently, as a special treat when Conrad was leaving to return to the city, Pearl made him promise that when he arrived back in town he would find a pizza shop and place an order to be delivered to their house in the forest. Pearl always chose an extra large, half pepperoni for Parsifal, and half ham and pineapple for her, claiming that they could save whatever was left for lunch the next day. Then they would wait with anticipation until at last, days— once even a week—later, a disoriented and bedraggled delivery person would find his way to their door, bearing a large, square box covered in dirt and leaves that contained an extralarge pizza. The pizza would be cold by then, and soggy, and usually the pineapple would have started to turn sour, but of all the meals Parsifal ever ate in the forest he cannot remember any he savored more completely.

Fountain pens are uncommon enough that it's not unusual for Parsifal to meet people—most often someone younger, but at times those his own age also, who should know better—who say, "Oh, I've never seen a pen like that. How does it work?"

Could that photograph on the wall of his room at the motel, the one of the family staring at the hole in the ground, actually have been of Parsifal and his parents? It would be surprising, considering how rare it was for Conrad to visit the forest. But if by some crazy chance it *was*, then what *was* the hole? Also, who took the picture? Needless to say, Parsifal had no memory of such a picture ever being taken, or looking down at a hole like that one, either.

Why *had* all the women been librarians? Parsifal can't begin to guess, though certainly in his first weeks out of prison, he spent most of his days among the library stacks and periodicals trying to adjust to his new life. Did the smell of paper remind him of trees?

Maybe, but it must have been more than that. Most likely it was the kindness of the librarians themselves. Parsifal imagined that, given the multitudinous variety of reprehensible human behavior represented on the shelves, his own qualities seemed less unusual. Or possibly the sight of a young man whose muscles had been hardened by years of living amid the forest, a young man whose shyness must have been a refreshing change from the bossy questions of senior citizens wanting help on their taxes and the rowdy teens the librarians were forced to discipline on a daily—no, hourly—basis, might somehow have stimulated in them a desire for intimacy.

He still remembered the first time he was seated at an oak table poring over books as closing time approached, and a sweet, bespectacled woman walked up behind him and started to massage his shoulders. After that, she inquired if he had a place to spend the night and, if not, would he like to come home with her?

Or maybe it was the scar.

In any case, the library was a welcome refuge after the notoriety of the Happy Bunny Preschool incident, and the harsh ways of the jail that had followed it.

On entering the forest, Parsifal almost immediately became lost. The first reason for this was that he had no idea at which edge of the forest the bus had deposited him. (For that matter, he hadn't been paying attention to which edge he was exiting from when he left years ago.) The second was that over the past twenty-five years or so there had been considerable growth in trees and bushes and such. And third, there must have been several changes to the boundaries of the forest itself, the pressures of real estate being what they were.

Even assuming that Parsifal was entering the forest at the exact point where he had left it, which was unlikely, there still was no telling if the perimeter was the same or, if it *had* shrunk, whether it was by feet or yards or miles. Also, third, or maybe fourth by now, Parsifal had to admit that even for a person raised in those woods—a person who once knew every plant, every path, each stream, and every largish rock—the passage of time had left each tree pretty much resembling its neighbor.

So this was his plan: He would simply enter where he was at the moment and keep going straight until he reached the other side of the forest. Then he would turn left and walk as far as he could, and then reverse himself at a slight angle to his right until he reached the end once more, and then reverse himself with a slight angle to his left, and so on and so forth until he spotted some familiar object, or possibly his old home itself. In other words, his path would look like this:

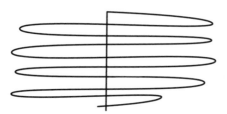

That was how it would work in theory, and of course it was his hope that he would not have to complete the entire sequence before he found the cup he was seeking. Unfortunately, however, Parsifal had no idea at all of the forest's real shape.

It could be a circle:

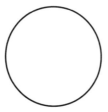

Or an oval:

Or even:

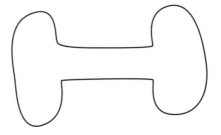

Or, troublingly:

Parsifal remembers Trellis once told him that, between worrying about library closures and the defacing of books by careless borrowers, she had had over one-third of her stomach surgically removed. Possibly because of this, she was extremely beautiful.

Here is a woman, Parsifal would tell himself as he gazed at the scar along the outside of her stomach, *who has lived in the world of shrinking budgets, of taxpayer shortfalls, of uncertainty, of the pressures of so-called public interest groups calling for the banning of books, and of major surgery as well, while I am still a child, relatively speaking.*

Parsifal thinks the dead twin back at the motel was named Omar, but he may have gotten it wrong. Omar may have been the other one.

VI

he fall was a good time to be searching in a forest. It wasn't winter, when everything was covered by snow, or spring, when all the new vegetation was the same distracting green, or summer, when there was so much growth that it was difficult to see anything at all. Plus there were a lot of bugs in summer. No, fall was when enough leaves had dropped away from the trees to allow for a slightly less impeded "line of sight," but there was still enough of a canopy to remind a person he was in a forest.

All around Parsifal, squirrels collected nuts and put them in places they'd remember later, while some birds, though not all, were packing up, shutting down their nests for the winter, and about to leave. In addition he was pleased to notice that the smell of warm decay so prevalent at earlier times of the year had been replaced by the pungent crispness of leaves crushed underfoot.

Circling above the forest were several birds, but due to the fact that there were so many of them, he couldn't say if one in particular had its eye on him.

For all Conrad's physical strength (and how can Parsifal forget the sight of him trudging forward with those fifty-pound sacks of cornmeal—even potatoes or chickpeas—on his shoulders—uphill, too—while balancing on slippery rocks as he crossed the small stream thirty yards or so from his home?), his father was not without what Conrad called "his mental phobias."

"I am ashamed to tell you, Parsifal," Conrad once said during one of their rare father/son talks, "about the irrational terror certain shades of yellow can provoke in me." Then he paused, and a look crossed his face as if suddenly he had forgotten how to write decimals or do addition.

"True, most of the time I'm fine, and most shades of yellow—that of lemons, for example, or even daisies—affect me not at all, but just let someone walk into a door wearing a tie or pair of socks dyed one particular, almost-greenish yellow, and your old dad has to choke down a scream and make up some ridiculous excuse to leave the room at once. Fortunately, son, occasions such as those, where panic completely takes over my body and I am reduced to an irrational state, are fairly rare."

After that, the conversation moved to something else.

The variety among librarians never failed to impress Parsifal. For example, Adele, whose job it was to maintain order in the "Teen Readers" section of the library, had sent to the hospital for stitches or with fractures more than one young person who had challenged her authority. And such was the level of respect accorded to Adele by the adult readers that her use of force had never once been questioned.

But with Parsifal, Adele was submissive, like a young adult novel whose pages he could dog-ear to his heart's content, on whose margins she invited his reader's notes. "Could you possibly raise your voice a little?" or "Could you possibly chew a little gum as we are being intimate?" he'd ask. And one evening Parsifal put a whole pack of licorice-flavored stuff into her mouth, pleased to see how happy she was to have it.

Not only did certain shades of yellow distress Conrad, but one day when the father and the son were taking a walk around their house to look at the fall foliage, his father began to tremble. "What's wrong, Dad?" Parsifal asked, but Conrad was unable to answer, only pointed to an ordinary brown caterpillar dangling from a thread suspended from a leaf.

"Caterpillars, too," was all his father whispered. Then, taking his father's hand, Parsifal led Conrad home as if he were blind.

A monster, also.

But this time it turned out that Parsifal had forgotten to pack his compass, an expensive model with glow-in-the-dark hands and a cover that snapped shut, a gift from a librarian he once knew. He *had* remembered to pack it on his visit to the florist, but somehow in between unloading his backpack and repacking it, the compass was left behind. Ordinarily, Parsifal didn't need a compass. He had a good sense of direction, but he also knew that in the forest it was hard to keep track of the sun because of the overhanging trees—a problem even in the fall—and much of the terrain was uneven, so the compass would have been really useful.

It was nearing noon, but Parsifal thought he would wait before stopping to eat his lunch. The toast and jam he'd had for breakfast had been surprisingly filling, and in the confusion following the death of Omar he had managed to carry away three jelly donuts, which he'd been nibbling on all morning.

Parsifal had once heard that love will find a way, but a compass would also have been nice.

Joe would have said that Parsifal had a subconscious desire to lose himself in his past, and maybe that was true.

So what if he did?

Parsifal passed what might have been a familiar waterfall, though it was impossible to be certain because waterfalls are particularly vulnerable to the changes of time and the seasons. This one, about six feet high, was probably nowhere nearly as forceful as it was in spring, or summer, with bugs hovering over the water, but it had a respectable flow. In the muddy edges of the pool at its base he could see the tracks of raccoons, deer, squirrels, and even a rabbit or two. This was their world, the forest; it was no longer his. He had given up his rights here when he left. Now that he had returned, blundering around like an oaf for no reason but his own selfishness, he felt ashamed.

I ought to go back where I belong, Parsifal thought, *back to the blind men and to my house, back to my small, owner-operated, pen repair business.*

But he did not.

Parsifal's favorite part of the library was the oversize-book section, which was off to one side, against a wall across from a large window. The reason he liked it was that the proportionately large size of the books made him feel like he was a child again, reading the books Conrad had brought him on those times when he chanced to pass a yard sale on his way to the forest. There had been the usual ones, like *Fighting Ships* and *Animal Buddies*, hanging from the bag on his father's belt, but out of all of them the one that was most special, left behind all those years ago, was *The Old Trapper's Guide to Wood-Craft.*

Everywhere he walked in the forest, Parsifal noticed that the birds, and sometimes even the insects, would fall silent. From the cheerful, continuous conversation they all seemed to be having, the moment he appeared they would become mute, as if they knew something about him they were not telling.

They had never done this in the old days, when he lived there.

"Unfit for life," the Germans call it.

For the first time, Parsifal wondered if Conrad too had taken the bus to the forest or if he had driven in his own car, which he would have had to park at the edge of the forest while he visited his family.

Until then, he had never thought of his father as driving anything.

But who exactly is fit for life?

Two hours later Parsifal settled himself on a warm, flat rock near the stream and opened the backpack that contained his sandwiches. They were in pretty fair shape, except for one where the mayonnaise had soaked into the slices of bread and made them soggy. He decided to eat that sandwich first and save the rest for later.

He wished he'd remembered the compass.

Along with the sandwich he had two carrots, and washed everything down with a drink of the tropical fruit punch he had filled his canteen with during the continental breakfast, which now seemed long ago.

Another reason Parsifal liked libraries so much was that in a library everyone was busy looking at the books and not at him.

Likewise, when he looked at a book, it did not look back.

Joe told Parsifal the following story: Many years earlier, while serving in the United States Army, he had been stationed at a remote outpost where the only available food had to be dropped in. Soon, he and his companions got tired of the usual canned and freeze-dried meals and began to crave something—nearly anything—that was fresh. One day Joe noticed a small stream near their base, and that night, using a spool of nylon thread, a branch, and some paper clips that had been tempered and sharpened, he assembled a makeshift fishing apparatus. The following day, using pieces of cheese and freeze-dried meat, Joe was able to return to his base with a dozen trout.

Of course, all of his fellow GIs quickly made the same type of apparatus, but for some mysterious reason Joe was the only one actually able to catch fish. As a result, his commander decided to give him a day off every week. On that day others did his chores and Joe did nothing but fish. "Some days I'd bring in twenty or thirty fish," Joe told Parsifal, "and the least I ever caught was ten, which was after a rain, so the water was muddy.

"Then we were transferred to an equally remote base, that, as fate would have it, also had a stream nearby. We tried the same thing, and do you know I never caught a single fish, though I could often see them swimming around in the water. Nor could anyone else. Nor have I ever been able to catch another fish to this day—not that I've tried all that hard."

"Why are you telling me this?" Parsifal asked.

"Just to illustrate a simple point: things change." Joe picked a jelly donut from a greasy bag, after offering one to Parsifal, and bit down. "Sometimes you can go back to what was, and sometimes, no matter how much you want to, you can't. Remember: whatever you do, don't look back."

Over the past several hours, Parsifal had felt one or both of his boots filling with water. This was because many of the areas of the forest had puddles that were covered by leaves and hard to see until it was too late. Naturally, this had also been true when he was young, but back then he was barefoot, and scarcely noticed it.

Now there was only one thing to do: keep walking until he reached dry ground again. When he did, he would sit on a log and pull off his shoes and socks, wring out his wet socks, and replace them with a pair of dry ones. The formerly wet, now just damp socks he would hang on the outside of his backpack to give them a chance to dry as he traveled.

It made him happy that he had thought to bring along so many pairs of socks, even if he had forgotten his compass.

He knew what Joe would say, but unfortunately Joe wasn't around to say anything to anyone these days.

Even if the whole forest *had* burned to the ground, Parsifal reasoned, the cup would not be destroyed, because it was made of metal, and though it might have lost some of its shape from the heat, it would still be there, though possibly trapped beneath a fallen tree or in several inches of ash.

For the first time it occurred to him that he should have brought along a metal detector to the forest, but it was far too late for that.

Sometimes Parsifal wonders if, when Pearl died in that forest fire, she felt much pain.

The first blind person he met when he arrived in the city was standing at a traffic light and carrying a white cane, but at that time a white cane and accompanying dark glasses meant nothing special to Parsifal. This was before jail and the Happy Bunny, even before he had finished high school. The colors of the man's shirt and pants did not match, and one of his socks was brown while the other was blue.

"How are you?" the man said, looking straight ahead.

"I'm fine. How are you?" Parsifal replied.

"I'm fine, too," the man said. Then the light changed and Parsifal crossed the street as the man remained standing on the curb. Parsifal had thought it odd, and when he recounted his experience to Mrs. Knightly, his social worker, she explained to him the man was blind.

"That white cane is a sure tip-off," she said as she rubbed some salve into his scar, "and sometimes you'll also see a dog with a handle on its back. Those are good indicators that the person you are looking at is unable to see."

Where there is love, there is sight.

By afternoon the forest had grown warm, though it was undoubtedly cooler than a treeless meadow or grassy savannah. Still, it was fairly hot for fall. As Parsifal walked up and down one hill after another, his face was often struck by stinging branches, and spiderwebs rubbed their creepy greetings onto his eyelids. He had forgotten about them since his old days of living there. He tripped over vines and sliced the top of one hand in a tangle of thorn bushes. Sometimes it felt as if he had never lived in a forest at all, but at other times the words of *The Old Trapper's Guide to Wood-Craft*, the book Conrad had given him, came back: *Don't run if you can help it. Make sure your fire is out. At the first sign of rain look for shelter. If lost, stand in one place and wait for help. Don't sit under a dead limb. Don't sleep beneath the tallest tree in a lightning storm.*

Parsifal *was* lost, but because he had expected that to happen, that part didn't bother him. He sat and ate a cherry Danish he'd taken with him from the continental breakfast earlier that day. It tasted good.

"Lost is only wanting to be somewhere you are not," the Old Trapper had written.

It was only after Parsifal had been thinking about the matter for a while that it occurred to him that all those people who had shared their breakfast with him that morning at the motel—the Danish couple, the twins' mother and father, and even the twins themselves— were, he would have to say, unnaturally small. It was hard to be sure about the children, true, but even they *seemed* far smaller than they should have been for children their age, although no one had actually told him the children's exact age, and certainly, after the accident that had killed poor, small Omar, Parsifal would not have been so callous as to ask how old the child was when he died.

And though at the time Parsifal had not crystallized his feelings about this size phenomenon (except, of course, that he *had* been conscious of feeling quite large in comparison to everyone else), it was only as he brushed the last crumbs of the Danish from his lap and prepared to take up his search for Fenjewla that he wondered: *Why had they all been so small?*

Also: *Was there a connection between the Danish he had just eaten and that old, spitting Danish couple?*

Probably not.

All day nothing fell from the sky to the earth, at least nothing that Parsifal witnessed. Had a truce been enacted? Could it be that news of such a truce had been announced while he was in the forest? Or, alternatively, was the sky merely reloading?

Lightning.

Jocelyn had worked in the reference section where Parsifal had come to find a certain article about button-filling fountain pens. It turned out someone had already checked it out, but one thing led to another, and the two of them talked longer than Parsifal had planned. One of Jocelyn's legs was considerably shorter than the other, but she made up for it with a thick sole on the shoe that went with the short leg. The result was an attractive, slightly wobbly step that caused her to lean her whole body into Parsifal's for support as she walked with him to the restroom to open it with the key kept behind her desk, because previously the place had been a sort of nexus for a brisk narcotics trade, ending only when a Thackeray scholar was found slumped over dead in a toilet stall from an overdose. Parsifal found Jocelyn's way of walking extremely attractive, and he told her so.

"Knock when you're finished," she said. "I'll let you out and lock the door after you."

When Parsifal had finished, and washed his hands and dried them using the brown paper towels from the dispenser, there Jocelyn was, standing outside the door, waiting for him with her key.

"Thanks," Parsifal said, and as they walked back to her desk, he noticed that in the process she bumped against him several times, supposedly by accident, but in a provocative way. Her hair was in a bun, and she wore glasses with a chain attached to the sidepieces so she could drape them around her neck and always find them. She smelled of orange blossoms.

"Anytime you need help," she said, "you can find me at the reference desk."

"I'm sorry about your limp," Parsifal said.

If the disintegration of thought into fragments is a sign of honesty, then does that mean the greater the disintegration, the larger the gaps there are between fragments, and therefore the greater the truth? And if so, then is a single fragment—no, the space between two fragments—the truest thing of all?

Parsifal.

It was his twelfth birthday when Pearl called Parsifal to her. He had been busy building a model out of mud and brambles of the city where his father worked. "Here," Pearl said, "I want you to have this."

She handed him a package made of bark and stood back as her son opened it.

Inside was a green tee shirt onto which she had sewn three golden anchors, one of them a little crooked.

"Do you like it?" his mother asked.

"It's beautiful," Parsifal said.

Along with the cup, he had also left the shirt behind, although by that time he had long since outgrown it.

Parsifal: *Perse à val.* Through the heart, pierced.

Parsifal passed through the forest, alert for any sign of the cup. The closest things he found were a few crushed beer cans and an empty container of insect repellant. *Not so bad,* he thought, *considering our current nation of litterbugs.* It was late in the afternoon. Soon he would need to stop and find a place to make camp for the night. One of the things he remembered from his lessons in woodcraft was never to wait until the last minute to make camp. "Spending a miserable night means the following day will be miserable as well," *The Old Trapper's Guide to Wood-Craft* had advised.

Then the earth opened about a dozen feet in front of him and an off-white washer-dryer combination, horribly deformed by the force of its impact, suddenly appeared to have risen out of a spot where there had only been a nasty patch of blackberries. Parsifal stared, and two things occurred to him: 1) that it probably had not risen, but crashed, and 2) if he had not taken a few moments earlier to change his socks, that might well have been the end of his search. Parsifal looked above him, peering through the hole the bulky appliance had created in the canopy of trees. The silhouette of a bird, or of a plane, passed noiselessly by.

He decided to make camp early.

When Parsifal first came to the city he was fourteen, and he noticed that city people expected him to be amazed by commonplace marvels. "What do you think of this?" they would ask, pointing to a telephone. Or, "Isn't that amazing?" they would exclaim standing in front of a blender when it was obvious *they* didn't think it was that amazing at all.

Parsifal's answer to most of these questions was that he didn't think much at all about the this-or-that they were asking after, nor did he find city life so very unusual, because he had been prepared for it by building cities out of mud back while he was still in the forest,

VII

 have completely ruined my life.

Parsifal once told Joe that in reference to the Happy Bunny episode, and Joe, to his credit, acknowledged there was some truth to this.

Except for fountain pens.

The night was growing cool. Parsifal sat beneath an over-hanging rock and ate a ham-on-whole-wheat sandwich and one of the apples he had packed. Still hungry, he fished out two of the croissants left from the motel's breakfast. They were a bit the worse for wear, but tasty nonetheless.

After supper he built a small campfire, more for companionship than anything else; its warmth was comforting and made him feel less alone. Despite the dry socks, his ankle was beginning to hurt. It had been many years since he'd walked this much.

Parsifal spread out his blue nylon sleeping bag and fell asleep with his feet close to the fire.

Sometimes, between visits, Conrad wrote Parsifal and his mother letters in blue ink on lined paper. The letters consisted mostly of such phrases as "I miss you," and "I wish I could come to see you," and "It must be nice in the forest this time of the year," but they seemed sincere. What *was* somewhat troubling, however, was the childish quality of his father's handwriting, something that Parsifal, even at a young age, was able to recognize, along with the man's numerous misspellings: *faduceary* for fiduciary, and *hege* for hedge.

One afternoon, as he and his mother were sitting outdoors on a log (having remembered to check for rattlesnakes), Parsifal asked his mother, "Do you suppose the people in the city realize what a poor speller my father is? Do you suppose they look at his handwriting and laugh?"

Pearl put her finger to her lips, as if she were about to impart some great secret. "I'm sure they don't. I'm sure they think your father is just fine. That's what he has a secretary for, among other things." Then she repeated "among other things," and her face darkened.

Pearl gave Parsifal his father's letters (and there were lots of them) so he could use them to trace the outlines of any unusual leaves he came across. He often brought leaves home, and in the evenings, cut out their silhouettes to pin to the walls of their house, though when he told Joe about this, Joe told him, "You were only attempting to gain control of a frightening environment." Parsifal wasn't so sure.

Conrad, he remembered, wrote in ballpoint.

Asleep in the forest that night, Parsifal dreamed he was flying over a different forest engulfed in flames. He flapped his arms as hard as he could, but he could feel them growing tired, and his altitude dropped. How long would it be before he plummeted into the flames? He couldn't tell because the smoke made it impossible to know exactly how far below the fire actually was. His eyes began to smart and the air grew hotter. Even inside his sleeping bag, he began to sweat. In his sleep, Parsifal could feel his feathers, or whatever made it possible to fly, burning. Finally he could barely flap his arms at all, and he began to fall extremely fast.

The bird, or drone, that had been following him had disappeared.

Parsifal would not have bought the house he currently owned, no matter how attractive the price (and it had been *very* attractive), had he known the house would be constantly surrounded by that circle of the mobile blind. True, the blind were not exactly missing from the neighborhood during the several visits he'd made when he was in the process of deciding whether to purchase the house. He would see a blind person, say, every second or third visit, but when he happened to ask the real estate woman if she believed it was the same person or different people she claimed not to know. Parsifal couldn't be sure himself, and afterward, when he asked a neighbor if this near-constant stream of blind men bothered him, the man only said that it would be worse if they could see. Still, they were always men, with canes and no dogs.

Why weren't there seeing-eye dogs? He'd read countless stories of such dogs pulling people from rubble and throwing themselves in front of runaway cars to save their masters. Did these men think they didn't need that kind of help? What did these men have against dogs that were willing to give up virtually their entire time on earth just to help out an entirely separate species? Parsifal knew there were dogs out there that had gone through months of training and were now waiting patiently to offer their aid; yet these particular blind men refused all canine assistance. How selfish could a person be if, even with poor eyesight, he couldn't take a minute out of every morning to open a can of dog food and dump it on some kibble? That's all the dog was asking for, Parsifal thought. That, and a bowl of fresh water. And walks, too, he guessed.

Parsifal wonders what Misty is doing right now. He wonders if she is wanting to use her pen.

A week after Parsifal had moved in and set up his pen cabinets and his shelf of inks, more blind people showed up. The minute Parsifal had put the last ink bottle on the shelf and stuffed his last pen wipe into the old Kleenex box where he kept them, the blind men all appeared at once, as if they had been lying in wait for him to complete his preparations. They brought their canes, too. But where had they been hiding? Had they been on a cruise, or at a seminar about the benefits legally due to them? Had they been able to see perfectly well while he was in escrow, but the minute escrow was completed they were suddenly struck by their affliction? The formerly friendly realtor returned none of his calls.

So there he was, the owner of a house that no one else would ever buy because of the tapping of the canes both day and night (for what was night to the blind?), and in addition, he wasn't even home to enjoy it.

Parsifal was not in the least opposed to the benefits that the blind, or anyone else, were entitled to.

And if, as they say, "Where there is love, there is sight," is it also true that where there is no sight, there is no love?

Parsifal was hungry. Fortunately he still had two sandwiches, a goose liver and a peanut butter and jelly, remaining in the bottom of his backpack. He thought he had packed more, but either he had eaten them during his sleep or they had fallen out of his backpack on his travels. Or, he supposed, the sandwiches might be sitting on the counter of his kitchen at that very moment, attracting ants, because he had forgotten to put them in the backpack. Along with his compass. He ate the goose liver and decided to save the peanut butter one for lunch.

Par/si/fal: Through the heart, pierced.

Parsifal followed the sandwich with a cup of water. Then, after burning the sandwich wrapper in what was left of his campfire, he rolled his sleeping bag and stuffed everything else into his backpack. He had read accounts of those who had returned to their childhood neighborhoods only to find them terribly diminished and shrunk to embarrassing proportions, but in his case, with the forest, the opposite seemed true. It appeared that the backdrop he had taken so much for granted while living there had grown. Either that, or he had shrunk.

Still, what else could he do but pretend everything was the way it had always been?

One day in the city Parsifal stopped a blind man. "Do you mind if I accompany you a while so I can ask a few questions?" he inquired.

This particular blind man was wearing an outfit Parsifal judged to be from the seventies: a Nehru jacket, bell-bottom pants, and a necklace with ceramic beads and an ankh, so Parsifal added, "That's a nice outfit you're wearing, though I don't suppose you can get a good look at it yourself." The man's hair was frizzy, too, in the style people used to call an "Afro."

But for some reason this blind man chose that moment to confront Parsifal. "Who asked you to come here and tell me what you think is nice or not? You think the opinion of a complete stranger is some sort of a gift, and that you are doing me a favor? I don't know you. I don't know what else you may like or not like. How would you feel if a necrophiliac said he finds you attractive? I can't even see how you are dressed, in order to have some possible basis with which I might interpret your so-called opinion, so why would I care what you think? Suppose you just walk back to wherever you came from and leave me alone, okay?"

"Well, okay," Parsifal said. "But for the record, I'm wearing a nice-looking plaid shirt, chocolate-colored cords, brown wingtip shoes, and an expensive wristwatch with a gold expansion band. Also, though you might not know what one is, I'm carrying a fountain pen, this one a classic Parker 51. So good luck on your lonely journey around the same block day in and day out, with that attitude of yours."

Parsifal stepped away. Actually he wasn't wearing any wristwatch at all, but he couldn't have stood letting the man get away with his superior attitude. Also, his chocolate-colored cords were actually jeans, and his shoes weren't wingtips. His shirt was plaid though, and he did have a Parker 51, though it wasn't his; he was on his way to deliver it to a customer.

Who was that person to judge? he thought.

Walking around the forest after breakfast, Parsifal saw that overnight there had been a shower of electric tooth-brushes. True, they weren't especially dangerous, and even if he'd been directly hit when they started dropping, it probably wouldn't have been serious because most of them had been deflected by the branches overhead. This was the first time, as far as he knew, that the choice of armaments had come from the bathroom.

And curiously, all the toothbrushes appeared to have been used. Their bristles were splayed, and some held preserved particles of old meals.

A librarian once described Parsifal's eyes as "twin wasps that had dug themselves into a mound of rancid suet in order to lay their eggs." They were making love beneath a display entitled "Nature's Friends and Foes," and even though the library was closed at that time, he did not think there was any way these words could have been intended as a compliment.

"And what do you know about laying eggs?" he asked her.

Her name was Ernestine. She wore her hair pinned up with clips on either side of her head, and once she had told him she felt betrayed over the loss of the file card system in favor of computers for keeping track of books.

"Is that all that's bothering you?" Parsifal asked.

"It's the metaphor as a whole I was reaching for," she explained, "and I'll thank you to keep my personal business out of it."

On the whole, Ernestine was far more patient than you might believe based on this exchange alone.

For lunch, Parsifal finished his last sandwich, the peanut butter and jelly. He decided he would search for the cup until it began to grow dark. If he found nothing, he'd go home the next day. Had he already decided that earlier? He thought so, but it wasn't important, and, strangely, it was that knowledge of an end in sight, as small as it was, that gave him the burst of energy he needed.

For one more day, anyway.

Once, waking at Ernestine's left side, Parsifal mentioned that the only dreams he ever had forecast his own death, but, he added, those dreams didn't happen very often. Ernestine's bed was in the shape of a boat and to climb into it a person had to use the rope ladder at the stern.

"Parsifal," she said, "surely you know by now that we all dream every minute of the night and part of the day, too, whether our eyelids are trembling under the thrill of REM sleep or are just propped open, as when we are waiting for our laundry to finish up in the dryer of a laundromat. Surely you know that the mind is too active ever to stop, because if it did, then so would we. Therefore I'm forced to say I don't believe you. The fact that your mind refuses to divulge what it's doing is not at all the same as you not dreaming. I'd say it actually indicates a deep insecurity of intimacy as well as a suspicious nature."

Ernestine paused. "Consider," she said, "last night I dreamed I was trapped in a soft-drink bottling plant, surrounded by giant-sized bottles all wrapped with coils of barbed wire. At the same time, you claim you were lying next to me, dreaming, you say, of nothing. Which of the two of us would *you* conclude is trying to hide something?"

Parsifal was about eleven or twelve years old when he found his first dead man in the forest. He had been practicing something Pearl liked to call "Numinous Consciousness," about which she had heard several years earlier from a tape Parsifal's father had brought her, along with a battery-operated tape recorder to play it on. What Numinous Consciousness meant was that a person could observe things from several points of view at once, including him- or herself. "I'm too old to start something as tricky as that," Pearl told her son, "but you, you're young and your mind is still flexible. I'll bet if you practiced for just a couple weeks you could get the whole thing down pat. I know it would make your father happy."

The process Parsifal was supposed to follow went like this: He was to sit down somewhere and imagine he was in the center of a circle, its perimeter maybe fifteen or twenty feet away. Then, point by point along that perimeter, he was to imagine what things would look like viewed from wherever that particular object was. On the day in question he was working on his fifth or sixth location when he spotted something shiny, which he couldn't actually have seen from where he was sitting, but from his new location the shiny object turned out to be a ring around a finger. Beyond that, there wasn't much to say. The body had been left outdoors enough that the smell was gone, and besides, living in the forest Parsifal had already seen his share of dead things, from deer to dogs to feral cats.

"I'm sure it isn't your father," was the first thing Pearl said when her son returned to tell her about his discovery.

"It's not a bad death, all in all," Conrad said, when he arrived a few days later and Parsifal took him out to see his discovery, "to be surrounded by the leaves and trees and beauty of the forest. Not bad at all."

The next time Conrad came back from the city, he brought along a shovel so he and Parsifal could dig a grave and lay the man to rest. Conrad took the ring, which turned out to be a nice-sized diamond, back to the city with him. He told Parsifal he would give it back to the man's relatives.

The whole experience made Parsifal consider.

By evening, Parsifal still had not found the cup. He was disappointed, but the good thing was that all his wood-craft had been coming back to him over the past couple of days. He was still lost, true, but he hadn't given in to panic so far, and that was winning most of the battle, according to the book, which added that there were far worse things than going without food for a couple of days. He tried to remember the map he'd left on the kitchen counter along with the compass. *The forest could not possibly be all that large, anyway*, he thought.

It was getting dark. Parsifal found another over-hanging ledge to keep him out of the wind, built a fire, opened his sleeping bag, and tried to fall asleep. It was going to be a long night, and for once he wished that he could pass the time dreaming.

He also wished he had a shirt with many pockets, such as he had seen the woman in the map store wearing.

That night the sky rained down a deadly assortment of commodes and sinks, and even a couple of claw-foot bathtubs, and Parsifal was glad to be safe beneath his ledge.

In his dream (possibly influenced by the shape of Ernestine's bed), he had rented a small, yellow, wooden rowboat and rowed out into the ocean, as far away from the shore as he could go. When he was finally exhausted, and could not possibly swim back, he took the axe he kept beneath the seat and chopped a hole in the boat's bottom.

Only afterward did it occur to him it would have been much simpler to dream of rowing a boat out into maybe ten feet of water and then jumping overboard tied to a concrete block. He didn't need to bring an axe along at all.

The Happy Bunny Preschool was somewhere in the dream as well.

No matter how many librarians Parsifal had been intimate with—and there were lots—he never confused the attributes of one with another. He was able to keep them completely separate, like books on different shelves, sometimes in different sections of the library entirely.

At one point, Parsifal saw a tree he thought he recognized. It was only an ordinary pine tree, with the usual bark, branches, and needles, but Parsifal had the distinct feeling he remembered it, because there were a few cones hanging right where he remembered them, and on one side where he remembered that a few of the bottom branches had been broken, they were barely attached and pointing at the ground.

Yet if that tree *had* been the same tree he remembered, it would have had twenty years more growth to it. In twenty years the broken branches surely would have fallen off, and the cones would have dropped and regrown twenty times.

His ankle was hurting more.

VIII

hen he was a child, Parsifal liked to climb trees, and spent many happy hours amid swaying tops, looking down on everything below: Pearl in her leather apron as she sat mending a shirt or stirring some stew or another in a pot, a shy deer stepping into a sunlit glade, a stalking fox, a prideful skunk, a timid rabbit, and a scolding squirrel. He observed them all without being observed. And although sometimes a branch would give way and he would find himself lying painfully on the ground, or at other times he got so comfortable that he dozed off and fell out of the tree, he would always climb back up and do it again the next day.

As earthbound as he had become of late, it was strange to think about those old days—*How free my life was back then*, he thought.

"And what's your obsession with librarians?" Joe once asked him. "Don't you ever date anyone but librarians?"

Parsifal thought about it. He supposed that for every hundred people or so who never dated a librarian, there must be at least one who had. And then for every thousand people, or ten or a hundred thousand people who had never dated a librarian at all (and didn't know what they were missing!), there had to be someone like him who had dated practically nothing but.

"I don't know," he said.

From where he was sitting, Parsifal could see that Joe had written the word *TRAUMA* on his yellow pad in big block letters and then made little wavy lines around it, pushing outward like flames.

"Okay then," Joe said. "I think it's time we got to that Happy Bunny thing."

Because after all, what sort of parent would send his or her child to something as ridiculously monikered as "The Happy Bunny Preschool," an institution that had based its entire identity on a single large and garishly painted children's slide with plastic bunny ears attached to the top and a set of yellowing foam tubes at the slide's base, apparently meant to represent whiskers? The slide was located in the front yard, only feet away from the street and within easy striking distance for any potential child molester or any car whose wheels left the pavement in an uncontrolled skid. What kind of parent *wouldn't* show more sense?

Were they some kind of monsters?

It was only noon, and already Parsifal was growing faint with hunger, despite the wisdom of woodcraft that reminded him starvation is what bodies were designed for. On the other hand, Parsifal also knew from spending considerable time in the reference section while waiting for Jocelyn to get off work that the human body wasn't designed to last much more than forty years or so. He was already on borrowed time.

His head ached and his ankle was sore. He needed to settle down to find a peaceful stream and then follow it out of the woods, because, as woodcraft had taught him, all streams lead to a lake or, better yet, an ocean. All he had to do was find one and to follow it, and then, when he hit the seashore, turn right or left, and sooner or later he would come to a port, maybe even to a nude beach.

Parsifal thought: *All I need is to find a stream.*

He seemed to be regressing.

Strangely enough, that very word, *trauma*, which Joe had so painstakingly written on his pad, was a reduction by about one-half of the phrase *humongous trauma*, which Parsifal's lawyer, Walter, had used to describe what he said Parsifal had suffered back in the forest, the very condition that, thanks to Walter, had allowed Parsifal to be released from the jail where he had been awaiting trial with only probation under the watchful eyes of a certified therapist following the Preschool Thing.

"You would like to see a real monster," Walter practically yelled at the judge (whose mother happened to be a children's librarian), "but instead you are looking at a poor victim, and the Parsifal standing here before you now is not a monster at all, but only the shell of the child who was eaten by the monster."

Which didn't make much sense to Parsifal, but Walter had told him never to interrupt when he was in the middle of summing up, so Parsifal sat quietly with his hands folded on the table. "You can either punish him for having been a victim or set this poor youth free (under supervision, of course) to find his inner child again." Walter winked at the judge and then sat down.

Parsifal couldn't tell if the judge had returned Walter's wink.

But also in Parsifal's favor was the testimony of the fire marshal who had spent considerable time analyzing the explosive qualities of the actual Happy Bunny plastic slide after which the school had been named. "It's only two steps away, chemically speaking, from the stuff used by terrorists," the man had told the judge, shaking his head in apparent disbelief. The marshal was dressed in a yellow slicker and black boots because, he explained, he never knew when he might have to leave for an emergency. He also described the stash of weapons and mostly pornographic photos—all heavily imprinted with the fingerprints of the preschool's director—that his firemen had discovered in the secret closet inside the director's office once the fire was put out.

In the end, with public outrage focused on the self-righteous German couple who had run the place—plus Walter's genius tactic of continually referring to the Happy Bunny's owner, Alf, as Adolf throughout the entire trial—Parsifal was practically hailed as a public servant, a person who, like an undercover officer, had just let things get a bit out of control in the course of his investigation. It happened all the time.

Also, given Parsifal's looks, the judge probably figured he'd been punished enough.

And as a matter of fact, who would have guessed the Happy Bunny Preschool didn't have a sprinkler system? Parsifal thought there must be building codes exactly for that kind of thing.

So, as it turned out, did the judge.

Among the many good effects of spending so much time in libraries was that Parsifal learned the Dewey Decimal System, so it wasn't long before Jocelyn and he could play little games while they waited for the library to close. For example, one night while waiting at his table by the newspaper rack, Parsifal wrote the number 127 and quietly left it on Jocelyn's desk when she was busy helping someone else. When he returned after that person had left, he saw that she had written beneath it "The Unconscious and Subconscious Mind," followed by the symbol for a happy face. That same night he was flipping through the pages of a pen magazine when out of the corner of his eye he saw Jocelyn behind her desk, holding up an index card with the number 716. Quickly, Parsifal found one of the scraps of paper they kept around the place and, using a stubby yellow pencil, wrote down "Herbaceous Plants." Then, pretending he was just another library patron, he brushed by Jocelyn's desk and dropped it where she might find it. When it was time to leave, Jocelyn signaled Parsifal by holding up a card with the number 021: "Library Relationships."

How Parsifal missed Jocelyn!

How sorry he was things ended the way they did!

One might well think that a person such as Parsifal, who was able to distinguish between the calls of a red-headed and a downy woodpecker, between a finch and a warbler, between the chucklings of a grouse and a partridge and a turkey, would have an excellent ear for music. Alas, this was not the case. Parsifal could barely tell a bossa nova from a symphony, a fado from a fandango, and yet as he walked blindly forward in search of a stream to help him find his way out of the woods, he was certain that he could make out most, if not all, of the words to Bob Dylan's "It's All Over Now, Baby Blue" coming from a dark spot in the trees before him—and sung not by the poeticizing master of rock and folk rock himself (what would *he* be doing in these woods at this time of year?)—or even in an amplified recording of his voice—but by three slurred and mostly off-tune voices, two men and a woman.

Parsifal staggered on in the direction of the sound, but the sound kept moving away. Either they were traveling rather quickly, he decided, or in his weakened state he was moving hardly at all. Then he walked around the trunk of a hickory tree and found them.

On the other hand, lightning.

Let's settle one thing now. All the small scars left from his day-to-day life in the forest are nothing compared to the one that bothers people most, the really big one, the one to which Walter was referring in the courtroom, the one Parsifal got on a weekend when his father happened to be there for a visit.

It was a night right after Conrad had arrived when he called Parsifal aside. "Parsifal," his father said, "your mother here and I need to discuss things such as your college education. Why don't you go off for the next few hours and practice woodcraft? I'd hate to think you were getting rusty."

So Parsifal followed his father's advice and had collected nearly a bushel of edible roots when it began to rain really hard. But that kind of downpour wasn't unusual, so he crawled into a hollow tree to wait. He figured the rain would let up in an hour or two, then he would go back home. He remembered that the Old Trapper had mentioned something about trees in rainstorms, but couldn't quite remember what, although concerning that particular tree there were, at least in retrospect, two important facts: first, Parsifal was grateful to be dry, and second, after about five minutes of being inside the trunk his hair stood on end and then there was a crack. That's all.

The next morning Parsifal woke split open from the top of his head down to the soles of his feet. He couldn't move, and around him the tree was still emit-ting smoke. He looked like an overripe plum, or maybe an overcooked sausage, or maybe a melon that had been left in the field too long, or an Italian squash that had grown too big—a giant zucchini beginning to burst apart.

Then he heard a voice that belonged to Conrad, who, sensing trouble when his son hadn't returned home by morning, had gone out to find him. He picked Parsifal up and carried him back to their house, where Pearl wrapped him in furs and animal fat and put him to bed.

"Get well soon," Conrad had said. "I'll see you in a while." Then he packed his briefcase, adding in the lunch Pearl had prepared for his trip back to the city.

It was a long time before Parsifal saw him again.

"Ouch," Joe said. "That must have hurt."

"It's the Pen Man!" Misty shouted. "Oh, wow!"

The fresh air of the forest and her good spirits had made her even more beautiful than before. Her skin shone beneath a glistening layer of perspiration, and her blouse clung to her body in an entirely natural, yet revealing way. She was also wearing something that looked like running shorts.

So, yes, the singing voices Parsifal had heard earlier that day belonged to none other than Misty and also—as she introduced to Parsifal her two friends—Cody and Black Dog.

"Far out," Cody mumbled.

Black Dog stared at his fingernails until, after what seemed an unusually long time, he added his own "Far out," as well.

"Pen Man!" Misty said. "Hey, what are you doing here? We were just—you know—taking a walk and a few things—and now you're here with us too. How did that happen?"

Black Dog stooped to pick up a marble-sized round stone and held it close to his face. Cody had caught some of his long light-brown hair in one corner of his mouth, was wetting it to a point, taking it out, studying it, then wetting it again.

"Pen Man," Misty said. "It's the Pen Man!"

"Are you all high?" Parsifal asked.

Misty giggled. "Pen Man. What are you doing here?"

He briefly explained that this very forest had been his old neighborhood for a time, and he had returned to find an article he'd left behind when he was forced to leave in a hurry.

"Like what?" Misty said.

"Maybe a potty," Black Dog offered. He and Cody saluted each other with high fives.

"Guys," Misty said.

The guys settled down, and Black Dog showed Cody the rock he had just found.

"Actually, it was a cup," Parsifal said.

"Yes, a cup. That's perfect," Misty said. "A cup is perfect. That's so great, a cup. Right, guys? Did you hear? It's a cup."

Cody waved both hands over his head like a boxer who has just won a bout, and it seemed to Parsifal that he was genuinely happy to hear the news. Black Dog, on the other hand, held the stone close to his eye, as if he were examining it through a nonexistent jeweler's loupe.

"And how are you doing with your search?" Misty asked.

"I'm afraid not too well. I've run out of food and I'm lost and just about ready to go back and call it quits."

"NO!" Misty shouted with surprising force. "You aren't allowed to do that! Guys—the Pen Man can't quit!"

To his credit, Cody appeared to give the matter some thought. He inserted his hands into the side pockets of his overalls and removed them several times, as if they might come out differently than they went in. He wasn't wearing a shirt, and hair stuck out of his armpits in two, surprisingly delicate light-brown fluffy patches. He looked fragile, all in all. "No, Pen Man," he said. "Misty's right. You can't do that."

Meanwhile, Black Dog was busy putting the stone into his mouth, sucking on it, and then removing it. After a while he would put it back into his mouth, and repeat the process. Parsifal wondered if the stone's taste reminded him of anything, but couldn't imagine what it might be, besides a stone. Black Dog said nothing, but nodded at him several times in a serious manner, to indicate that he was in complete agreement with Cody and Misty.

"Wait," Misty said. "I have an idea. We all have extra energy bars I made myself for our trip to the forest. Guys, if we could each take two of the kind we like the least and give them to Pen Man here, then he'd have"— she paused for a moment—"a total of six energy bars that he could use to help him while he looks for his cup." Misty turned to Parsifal. "Then, when you find your cup, you can fix my pen that you've already been holding for a long time. Here. I'll start with a chocolate-cherry and a granola-cocoa. Cody?"

Cody fished around in his pockets to find a banana-apple and a prune-sesame bar. Black Dog tossed in two peanut-fig clusters.

"Thanks," Parsifal said. "Actually, your pen's been ready for a while. I think you'll be pleased with the result."

"That's great—really good news. Then that's that," Misty said. "You'll go on, you'll find your cup, and when you come back, then you can show it to me, and I'll finally get my pen back." She brushed her hair away from her face. Her hair seemed to have found some extra golden highlights since he had last seen her.

"I have a good feeling about this, Pen Man." She dug into her waist pouch and handed him a stick of gum. "You may as well take this, too."

"It's Parsifal," Parsifal said.

"What?"

"Parsifal is my name."

"Well, okay, whatever. And now we have a few things to do yet before we go back, so Cody and Black Dog and I have to be moving on, if you don't mind." She paused. "Listen," she said, "it was amazing meeting you out here like this—almost like it was meant to be. I think this could be really important for you, Pen Man. And not just for you, but maybe for a lot of other people, too. Do you ever have the feeling the things you do mean something? I mean in addition to the things you think they mean?"

"Sometimes," Parsifal said.

"Me too. So you be careful, like I said. I'll see you when all this is over. Don't blow it, Pen Man—Parsifal. Okay?"

Then Misty stretched out her arms as if she were flying and ran on ahead, with Black Dog and Cody following.

Parsifal looked down. At his feet was the round stone that Black Dog had been sucking on, lying wet and shiny on the ground. For no good reason whatsoever Parsifal bent down, picked it up, wiped it off, and stuck it in his pocket.

"Sand," he had answered Joe.

You might think that a person as sensitive to the scrutiny of others as Parsifal would be happy to be surrounded by blind individuals, but this was not the case. In a certain way, whatever gasps his external appearance may have provoked among many sighted individuals (with the notable exception of librarians), he was still left with the comfort that the person who had made such a quick and superficial judgment of him was unable to see beneath his skin to his real, more complex, and creative self.

Conversely, Parsifal's difficulty with the blind was that he was unable to blame their judgments on any misperception. They, by virtue of not having to depend on externals, were able to plunge straight into a person's soul, and, like long-deceased Aztec priests, seize the living hearts of their victims (in this case, him) and rip them out. In other words, Parsifal thought, *How would you like it if your place of residence was encircled day and night with a ring of dead and judgmental Aztecs?*

It was after high school that Parsifal—having run out of such benefits as his social worker had gotten for him, and run out of Mrs. Knightly, too (she got married)—alone and, like so many other high school graduates, without a skill or means of supporting himself (he hadn't yet discovered fountain pens), chose the crawl space of the Happy Bunny Preschool to make himself a little temporary shelter. It had been a damp day and cold as, curled in the cramped crawl space beneath the schoolroom, surrounded by spiders, rodent droppings, and years of toddler trash, Parsifal suddenly remembered his life back in the forest and the comfort that even a small fire could bring. And so he heaped atop a base of Popsicle sticks a pile of discarded chocolate milk cartons, plus a few pages torn from old coloring books, and struck a match. The cartons, coated as they were with wax, flamed up with a surprising intensity.

The bird circled above, and he was almost positive it was the same one he had seen a couple of days ago, though it was hard to know with birds, considering that they pretty much look alike. Ditto a drone painted to look like a bird.

The librarians in the county jail, he quickly learned, were not to be trusted.

Actually, when Parsifal stopped to think about it, he didn't even know why that cup was so important, although Misty seemed to agree. Still, what was broken can never be fixed completely—he had learned that from fountain pens. What was broken can be replaced, true—but fixed, no. Or it can be repaired; that is to say, the damage can be halted at a certain point, but once it has already happened, nothing can be reversed. Nothing can be made as good as new. Although a nib can be replaced with a new one, there's always something slightly different—sometimes better, sometimes worse—but not the same. Never the same.

He just *has* to get that cup.

One of the first things he noticed when he arrived in the city was that dogs, especially seeing-eye dogs, barked at him far more than at other people. Trained to be calm under all conditions, these helpers of mankind would nonetheless tug at their harnesses as if to pull their masters from harm's way as he passed, although Parsifal meant no harm. It wasn't his scent, because after he had washed several times they continued to do it. His best guess was it was something else.

Fenjewla.

If a person will only think about it, the first fountain pen was undoubtedly the human body itself, with its seemingly endless (till death do us part) supply of ink. So it's not at all hard to imagine some cave person sitting around after a hunt and noticing that he had pricked his finger on a thorn, or maybe even had the tip of his finger bitten off by a wild animal, then discovering he could use it to draw pictures.

Parsifal believes no instrument is more expressive of our bodies and ourselves than a fountain pen in proper working condition. Not the messy brush of painters; not the smudgy smears of charcoal or pencil; not the childish crayon; not the soulless ballpoint so favored by Conrad; not the greasy roller ball; not the unpleasant, percussive smack of typewriters (now mercifully almost extinct); certainly not the silent, eyeball-straining pixels of the computer screen.

And yet, of course, therein lies the downfall of the pen, for what *are* the letters formed by a fountain pen, whether exact and inerasable or smeared by some careless thumb, but two-dimensional replicas of our three-dimensional selves, our weaknesses to be exposed to the world by the most amateur grapho-analyst, our spellings and misspellings (Conrad!) mirroring the shallowness of our thoughts, the carelessness of our actions, the foolishness of our hopes, leaving behind a record of us for all to see, for all to judge and to find lacking, unlike the bland and infinitely correctable historical record of the computer-generated page.

Yes, better to write nothing at all, Parsifal sometimes tells himself, *to vanish without a trace rather than to produce such an Everest of incrimination, such an effluvium of ridiculousness*. Yet what else, after all, is there, either exposed for all to see or hidden?

So, is it any wonder that fountain pens, those faithful transcribers of our frailty, are rapidly losing favor to the monstrous aphasia of this world in general?

There's no need to answer that, he thinks.

Effluvium?

It occurs to Parsifal that if he can find one single tree from his childhood—its bark, its leaves, its height, its width, the way its branches fork out from the trunk, the way its roots reach into the ground, its age, its health, the colors of the bark, the colors of the leaves, the tops and bottoms of the leaves with the veins that feed them, their textures, the texture of the bark, the smell of the wood, the sound of the air moving through the branches and the leaves, the creaking of the branches in the wind, the shadow the tree throws upon the ground, the sorts of animals that are a part of the tree, from the bark beetles to the cicadas to all those other insects, some of which might be suspended from its branches in cocoons or have laid their eggs directly on the branches themselves; if he can describe the size and shape of the eggs, the birds too, and mammals if there are any, and what *their* houses look like, their nests, their dens in its roots—and notice here he's not even talking about those branches that have been broken and how they might heal, or which are beginning to sprout, or which have holes drilled into them by birds and if there are any spiderwebs or tents left by bag worms or other moths, and if there are any vines, and how thick the tree's leaves are, or how far its branches extend from the trunk and whether they are narrower or wider at the top than at the bottom, and (he almost forgot one of the most important things of all) whether it has nuts, or fruit, or flowers—if he can just find that, then he could turn right around and not have to find a cup at all.

Is wanting to possess anything at all that lasts—compared to the greater truth of change embodied in trees and animals—just vanity?

"All is change," Joe would say.

Then again, he thinks, *so what?*

It was after the whole Happy Bunny experience, when Walter's defense—improbable as it seemed—had worked and Parsifal was at his first court-mandated visit, that Joe told Parsifal he didn't like to judge people.

"I suppose that's why I became a therapist, Parsifal," Joe said, "because for me, no matter how much blood you may or may not have on your hands, you're just another struggling human being. Believe me, I've worked with plenty of criminals, and by now nothing would surprise me."

Not surprisingly, therefore, judgment-wise, Joe's own appearance ranged from neglected to downright shabby. He favored Hawaiian shirts, half tucked in and half out, and mostly went around unshaved. He was also completely bald, giving him the look of a giant woodchuck. And yet, Parsifal had to admit that Joe tried to be helpful.

"You don't have to be so hard on yourself, Parsifal," Joe said during one of Parsifal's early visits. "Anyone can see that there's a straight line from your mother perishing in that raging forest fire to you burning down the Happy Bunny by 'accident.' *Fire—get it?* Now think of your own life as a sentence being written by someone not unlike yourself. What you've already written:

everything from the past—say, from your mom and the forest fire, until this moment—has filled up many pages. And trust me, those blank pages ahead are your future. Remember that they are the ones you have to fill out—and no skipping because of drugs or inattention."

Parsifal thought about it and frankly was unable to see Joe's point, though he didn't want to disappoint the man by saying so. He had never taken drugs, even once. Joe scratched the side of his face near his mouth, where a spot of egg from his breakfast had stuck.

"Say," Joe added, "I just thought of this now, but you don't suppose your mom set the fire on purpose, in order to cover up her murder of your dad for his infidelities during his life in the city, do you?"

Parsifal considered. It was possible, of course, but he couldn't see how Pearl would have gotten by without those sacks of beans and rice Conrad used to carry into the forest for the two of them. He said, "I doubt it."

"Well, it was just an idea," Joe said. One of his better qualities as a therapist was that he never seemed overly attached to his theories. "But say," Joe continued, "here's another one: Have you ever thought of going into the fountain pen repair business? It won't make you rich, but it's a steady income, plus you could work at home."

Parsifal noticed that the fingers of Joe's right hand were stained with dark blue ink, the result, he now knew, of an ill-fitting feed. Joe crossed his legs. He appeared to have walked through something unpleasant on his way to the office, and some of whatever it was had stuck to the soles of his huaraches.

"That's an interesting idea," Parsifal had told him. "As a matter of fact, I've already started."

Parsifal ate the prune-sesame bar, which was not nearly as bad as it sounded, and it filled him with a *surprising* amount of energy. He did not know what Misty and her friends had put into those bars, but this one was dynamite. He walked and walked. He searched the ground for any signs of home (a flattened door, a heavy iron skillet). He looked above his head (for maybe a familiar low branch he used to loll on, now raised up by time), but saw nothing he recognized. Was something burning? Had Misty and her friends made a small campfire to toast drugs, or was this smell part of a larger conflagration, possibly hundreds of miles away? He could not tell, except that his nostrils tingled in a way that made him nervous.

Joe had been right; Parsifal did not have a good history with fire.

So his first thought was to flee, until he remembered the advice of the Old Trapper: if a person is uncertain of the source of a fire, the worst thing to do is run, because the person might race straight toward it and by the time the person realized this, he or she (!) would be too tired to outrun it. Observe the birds, the Old Trapper wrote, because the birds are the ones who have the best overall view. See from what direction the birds are flying; watch where they are headed.

Great advice, except for the fact that all the birds had disappeared completely, including the one that had been circling or spiraling overhead, it seemed, forever.

Pearl.

IX

arsifal must have been nine or ten years old when Conrad took him aside one afternoon to explain the intricacies of double-entry accounting. They sat together on an old log, his father in his dark, pin-striped city suit with a tea towel covering the log so he wouldn't get his pants dirty, and Parsifal in his usual knockabout outfit of shorts, a tee shirt, and, sensing a cold front was on its way, an animal pelt or two that Pearl had stitched together in her spare time.

"To begin with, son," Conrad said, "in double-entry accounting every transaction is recorded by entries in at least two accounts. The total of the debit values must equal the total of the credit values, and the premise for this is that any monetary transaction must logically affect two aspects of a company." Parsifal must have looked puzzled, because his father continued, "For example, if an item is purchased—I call it the 'debit inventory'—then it must also be paid for, and I call this part the 'credit bank account.' That's the first aspect. Are you with me so far?"

Parsifal nodded.

"Alternatively, if an item is sold, something I call the 'credit inventory,' then the company must also be paid for it out of the debit bank account, and that's the second aspect."

"That seems only fair," Parsifal told him.

"Yes," Conrad answered, "it is. But you might also note that while most transactions consist of two entries, some may have as many as three or more entries. For example, a supplier invoice total equals the net value plus the taxes. This system is called 'double entry' because all transactions must 'balance.' That is, at the end of the day when you reach for your jacket to go home— not to your house where you live with your mother here in the forest, you understand, but to a place like the modest pied-à-terre I am forced to maintain in the city all the while I am missing your mother and you—the debit and credit sides must equal the same amount." Conrad gave his son an encouraging smile.

"Historically, debit entries have been recorded on the left-hand side and credit values on the right-hand side of a general ledger account, but of course once you get the hang of it you are free to express yourself in any way you wish."

Then Conrad handed Parsifal a large pile of acorns and told him that they were his inventory. "Now," Conrad said, "even though I just gave you those acorns, I want you to sell some of them back to me at a nickel each so you can make a profit. But at the same time, I want you to know I'm going to be charging you for delivering the acorns to you just now, and also you are going to have to pay me rent for that flat spot on top of this log where you have put them. And by the way, even though I'm going to be paying you for those acorns, every so often I will cheat you, and you won't be able to stop me. It might very well be that your bookkeeper is embezzling some of your profits; perhaps he or she is a gambler, or has a pet charity, but you won't know that until the end, when you will be able to make a full accounting by means of the technique I am about to teach you."

In addition to the acorns, Conrad gave Parsifal two pens, a ballpoint with red ink for the debit part, and another ballpoint with black ink for the credit part. There was something elemental there, something irrefutable, Parsifal thought. So they spent the afternoon, Conrad buying acorns and Parsifal keeping track of them, and by the end Parsifal owed his father sixty-five cents and had a pretty good idea of the fundamentals of such bookkeeping, which eventually, in the years that followed, he used to run his fountain pen repair business.

At his trial, Parsifal's case was also helped by the parents of one of the children who had been blinded in the fire. They appeared in court dressed in modest clothing—the mother in a blue dress with fringe on the bottom and the father in a green blazer and red tie—and they brought with them their daughter, Bronwyn, whose eyes were still covered by gauzy white bandages.

"We're Christians and we believe it's our duty to forgive—and besides," they told the judge, "it wasn't looking as if Bronwyn was on the way to turning into much of a reader."

"Thank you," Parsifal mouthed to them across the room.

"God bless you," they mouthed back.

The rest of the morning Parsifal spent walking. His energy level remained high, thanks to whatever ingredients Misty had tucked inside that bar, and he knew he had five more left that were like it. He felt confident. He didn't know if the smell of smoke was diminishing or if he was just getting used to it, but it wasn't a concern at that moment.

So Parsifal had just walked into a small clearing, maybe thirty yards in diameter, with some berries and wild
flowers still in bloom, when there was a terrific whooshing sound above him, and he looked up in time to see
something very large strike the ground at the far side of
the clearing. He ran to where it had hit, and there, nearly
unrecognizable at the bottom of the crater it had made
in the soft ground, was a 1957 Chevy Impala coupe,
painted powder blue with a white top, the largest object
he had ever seen fall from the sky. What did it mean,
he wondered, that who or whatever was dropping these
objects onto the earth would let go of a classic like that?

Clearly, far from dying down, as Parsifal had hoped,
the intensity of the combat seemed to be increasing.

Another time, Parsifal was sitting around talking with
his therapist, Joe, in his office. It was in the evening, well
after Joe's usual hours, because Parsifal had missed the
previous three appointments for some reason or another,
and Joe had left a message to say he was beginning to get
worried and might have to report Parsifal to his probation officer if he missed any more. When Parsifal called
him back, Joe said he was still at his office, just finishing
up some paperwork, and he'd be there if Parsifal wanted
to drop by right away. Joe said he was about to order
some Chinese takeout, and added that if Parsifal wanted

to split the meal with him they could talk together over supper. Joe told him that he was thinking of won ton soup, mu shu pork, kung pao chicken, and some special fried rice. How did that sound?

It sounded good, Parsifal told him, but he thought it might be a good idea to order some vegetables as well, and maybe some egg rolls and beans in garlic sauce wouldn't hurt.

Joe agreed, and said that Parsifal should hurry. If the food arrived before Parsifal did, he would save a copy of the bill so they could split it.

Parsifal arrived just as the delivery person, a middle-aged man with a heavy mustache and an accent full of the scornful pauses an overeducated person in a foreign country will often interject, was leaving. Joe showed Parsifal the bill and they divided it, including the tip. The won ton was too salty and, Parsifal suspected, laden with MSG, but the mu shu pork was fragrant and tender, and the chicken was a revelation of dry spiciness combined with smoky chicken flavors. The rice and egg rolls were average, and the beans were overcooked.

"What can you expect from takeout?" Joe asked. "And besides, don't you think you're a little picky for someone who was raised on the floor of the forest eating God-knows-what?"

When they finished, they opened their fortunes. Joe's was "You are a pleasant person and others find you

easy to relate to." Parsifal's was "Darkness lies ahead."
They shoveled the dirty plates and containers into a
trash bag that Joe put outside his office door.

"The cleaning person will dispose of it," Joe said, as
Parsifal settled into his usual chair and Joe took his.

"Say," Joe began, apropos of nothing, "I don't suppose you happen to have a picture of your mother in
your wallet or anything like that, do you?"

"In fact, I do," Parsifal answered. "I carry one of her and
me that my father took. I must have been three or four
years old, and Pearl would have been in her early twen-
ties." He fished around inside his wallet and handed the
picture to Joe. In it, Pearl was wearing her short, light-
weight, summer deer-hide skirt and a black Frederick's of
Hollywood bra. She was posed on a tree limb, maybe ten
feet off the ground, so the picture angled upward, revealing her long, tanned legs. With one arm she was holding
on to a vine, about to swing off into space, as with the other she grasped Parsifal's waist to take him along with her.

"Wow," Joe said. "What a babe your mother was. I'll
bet you had a few lustful thoughts along that line."

"Probably," Parsifal said. "But no more than average
for a kid. After all, she was still my mom."

"Hmm," Joe said. "Do you mind if I make a copy of
this for your file?" He walked over to the cheap copy
machine in the corner of his office, took a pile of paper
off the top, and put in a quarter.

"Go ahead," Parsifal said.

The machine whined for a while and, after about a minute, a copy wriggled out.

"What about your dad?" Joe said. "Does it seem at all odd to you that you haven't really made much of an effort to contact him since you left the forest and moved to the city where he's supposed to work? Or, for that matter, wouldn't you think that with all the publicity surrounding the Happy Bunny tragedy that he would have attempted to contact you?"

Parsifal thought about it. "When I first arrived here, mostly I was concerned with survival. Insofar as the preschool was concerned, I imagine he might well have been embarrassed."

"Hmm," Joe repeated. "And since then?"

"Well," Parsifal answered, "I guess what with me starting my own pen repair business at your suggestion and all, my dad just hasn't been a priority for me. By the way, I meant to tell you that the pen repair business is coming along pretty well, even though it's still in the early stages."

"Glad to hear it," Joe replied. "But let this be a warning: It seems very likely to me that you are now in the process of beginning to confuse me with your father. This is called transference, and it's a pretty common thing in the analyzing profession, something we analysts see every day. I'm not sure what you can do about it, but the main thing for you to remember is that if this transference between your father and me is ever actually completed, then our therapy will have to come to an end."

"I don't think there's much danger of that," Parsifal said. "For one thing, Conrad dressed very differently than you."

"Yes," Joe said, "I expect he did."

Who was it that said our sole glory as humans is to leave behind a record of our crimes and desires?

Using a fountain pen to do it.

Climbing a small hill, Parsifal stops for a moment to catch his breath; he must have been almost running in the forest without even knowing it. *Watch out*, he tells himself. *If you injure yourself in this wild spot, it might be curtains.* Beneath him, he can't see more than a hundred yards in any direction. The leaves of some of the trees are starting to turn various colors, and above him the sky is starting to assume its winter blue. The bird has returned (or never left), but is higher than ever.

He wonders if Misty is having sex with Cody or Black Dog. Possibly, seeing as she appears to be under the influence of drugs, and anything can happen under those conditions. His heart begins to race. For that matter, seeing as drugs are in the picture, why not with both men at the same time?

Parsifal can feel his face turn hot.

He walks back down the hill. He has to find that cup.

Parsifal supposes that trudging through the woods, hour after hour without any signs of hope, might be discouraging to many people, but for him, alone again in the woods, it seems almost as if his scars, from the fire and other things, have disappeared, except, of course, for the mark left by lightning.

His ankle feels a little better.

With Cody *and* Black Dog?

When Parsifal thinks about blindness, he thinks about all the ways that people can lose sight: some at birth, some later, slowly or all at once. Others lose it, then get it back again, then lose it forever. And just as the way in which blindness arrives must inevitably alter its effect, surely the varieties of not-seeing must differ as well. Some see black, others purple, red, explosions of color, and possibly even experience moments when the curtain between the eyes and the world is parted for an instant, then comes crashing shut again. Or things may dissolve over weeks or years, like a dark lozenge left in a glass of water, until over time the actual lozenge is invisible, a part of the now-dark water. Or the field of vision may become covered with spots, like splotches on a shower door, until it's impossible to see if there's anyone else there in the bathroom along with you. Or that same field, once large, may start to shrink, like the closing credits of a cartoon, a circle growing smaller until nothing's left but a dot, then black.

So Parsifal had been walking and thinking this and that, when suddenly he came upon a sight that stopped him cold: a rectangular hole in the ground, about three feet wide and six feet long. It looked to be about two feet deep and was not the result of any falling object. *Or that's the way it is now*, he thought, with increasing excitement. Twenty or so years ago the hole would have been deeper, empty of debris, the sides steeper, and the bottom filled with the sort of deadly pointed stakes that he himself had pounded in as a child, the sharp ends pointing upward.

Twenty or so years ago it would have been a perfect trap for catching a deer that, walking down its usual trail, would not have noticed that a pit had been dug there overnight and covered with branches and leaves so it looked the same, except for the pile of dirt to one side, as the rest of the forest floor. Then the deer, as frequently happened, would stumble in and be unable to get out. The following morning, or next day, or the day after that, Parsifal would find the unfortunate animal, usually still alive, impaled on the pointed stakes he had set in the ground and in terrible agony, and he would dispatch it with a rock. After it had finally ceased to move, Parsifal would lower a ladder made of sticks to climb down and lift it out. Then he would drag its body back to Pearl, who would skin and cook it for their dinner. She said that living in the forest had made Parsifal strong for his age.

His infinite wisdom.

It was not just the odd deer he caught, either, because, skilled in woodcraft as Parsifal was, he frequently helped his mother by making snares for small animals (rabbits, possums, and squirrels) and deadfalls for medium-sized ones (raccoons and badgers and the occasional fox). But now, finding what may well have been a pit that Parsifal himself had dug twenty years ago meant two important things: First, that he *was* in the right forest. Second, the location of his old house must be nearby, because even as strong as he had been in those days, he still tried to dig his pits so his victims would be within easy dragging distance of home.

Parsifal had to be sure, however. Carefully, he lowered himself down the sides of the pit to the bottom, where, much as he expected, he sank another few feet into the collection of leaves and branches that had collected there over the past two decades. Were there pointed stakes? He had avoided them by staying close to the walls, but now he reached toward the center and fished around beneath a pile of debris. Yes. His fingers closed carefully around what seemed to be a pointed stake, and he carefully tugged it out of the ground. The point had been dulled by time, and the bottom had almost completely rotted away, but there it was. He was the person who had dug that pit, and sharpened the stakes, and lined the bottom. This pit was his.

When Parsifal climbed back out, he was exhausted. He spread his sleeping bag out there and then, alongside the pit, built a small fire, and, still clutching that rotting, formerly so-pointed stick, fell straight asleep.

That night Parsifal dreamed he bit into a fortune cookie that was full of blood.

Encouraged by the discovery of the pit, Parsifal woke, put out his fire, ate another energy bar—a fig and peanut variety—and began his search anew, springing up hills and bounding down them again, rapidly intending to conform to the following plan:

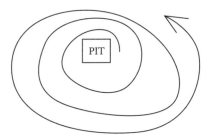

The forest raced by in a whirl of brown and green, tree trunks and leaves, bushes and grassy patches, and little creeks filled with rocks, and crawfish and tadpoles and newts. He didn't know what Misty had put in those energy bars, but they packed a wallop, and it wasn't until a couple of hours had passed that he realized that not only did he have no idea where he was, he couldn't even tell if he had already searched the section he was presently occupying. Whatever that was.

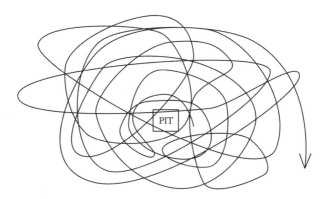

He scanned the ground, hoping to find another pit, but found none, not even the hole he had slept alongside.

At lunchtime, even though he wasn't particularly hungry, Parsifal made a small fire in a clearing and brewed a cup of tea in order to get his bearings. It is just for this reason—and also because it's light and easy to pack—that tea is one of the most essential items for any backpacker. He was glad to have remembered it. Sipping his tea, he took stock of his situation: On one hand he had three—no, four—energy bars left, but on the other hand, he was still completely lost. He finished his tea and felt calmer. Above him the same bird, or birdlike creature, was still circling, or maybe spiraling, down and back up again.

Then Parsifal had an idea—not a logical plan, certainly, but what good had logic done him anyway? None at all, was the answer. So—and even he had to admit this was a reach—if his eyes had failed to produce the desired effects, what would happen if he continued his search without them, if only for a while? Suppose, he wondered, he blindfolded himself and walked around for a bit? He thought of the blind men in his neighborhood. Without the distraction of sight would some deeper sense take over—smell, or hearing, or even taste? Well, possibly not hearing. Would he somehow be transported back to some earlier, wiser, childhood-self? There was only one way to know, and though it was slightly dangerous, true, it was also less dangerous than, say, crossing a busy street in the city without looking to the right and to the left, blindfolded or not. And after all, he could always take the blindfold off at any time.

He cut himself a stick so he could feel his way before him and wrapped a bandana around his eyes. *Okay, Parsifal*, he told himself, *go forward, but be careful*. You don't want to fall into a pit like that second man you found when you were young, not so many days before—come to think of it—the disastrous forest fire where you left your mother, Pearl, behind forever, as she stood there coughing and bravely waving good-bye.

Misty + Black Dog + Cody = ?!

Despite his scar, or possibly because of it, you might be surprised how many people, once they get over their initial shock at his appearance, ask him, "Parsifal, in your opinion what is the best pen for me?"

"Ha, ha," Parsifal usually laughs to put them at ease. Then he continues: "Well, that's a difficult question, and one that demands more information than what you've provided me. In other words, outside my firm belief of the superiority of a pen which draws in its ink supply by means of a piston, and that preferably also has a window to view the ink supply through, the question of which is the pen for you depends largely on what sort of writing you actually do. Also your favorite color. Here, by the way, I am putting aside the question of what is the most comfortable size and weight of a pen, which I advise you to discover for yourself by cutting several dowels of varying width and experimenting not only with how they feel in your hand but also by tying small weights (ordinary fishing sinkers will do nicely) on to them to find what is most enjoyable.

"Once you know what size is good for you, the rest depends on the sort of nib you prefer much more than the actual pen. Nibs run from fine (and extrafine) to broad and extrabroad. If you are an accountant, for example, and require neatness and the ability to squeeze several numbers into a relatively small space, then you might prefer an extrafine. On the other hand, if you are a high-powered executive who spends many hours of the day signing various documents, you may well enjoy a broad nib, one that will make a bold impression and say, *Yes, I have signed this and I have a whole raft of high-priced lawyers at my beck and call who are all waiting to sue your ass off.* That is, unless the document is of an incriminating sort, in which case you should probably borrow someone else's pen."

At this point usually one of two things will happen. Either the person Parsifal is instructing will pull out a piece of paper and take feverish notes or he or she will turn slowly away, so as not to alarm Parsifal by any sudden movements, and leave. The second is the choice that most make.

If they do stay, however, sooner or later Parsifal will add that one of the other benefits of being a fountain pen user is that not only does a person have a greater variety of tips to choose from in terms of line width, but he or she also has a choice between round-tipped, oblique (as with Misty's Waterman), and stub, a nib that is exactly like it sounds, cut off at the end to make a sort of spade, a satisfying nib to write with for the workmanlike slap it makes against the page, even though it may well be less agile than the traditional rounded tip. "Nibs," he is sure to add at this point in the conversation, "also vary from flexible, meaning those that produce a greater line variation, to firm or stiff. In addition, you can find them in steel, gold, and titanium—even glass—although, the most popular is gold."

This isn't word for word what Parsifal will answer each and every time, but it's fairly close.

A pit to catch an animal. A deer, for example.

"In my experience," Parsifal tells those who ask, "there are two kinds of people: those who enjoy complications and subtlety, and those who do not. If you are not the sort of person who enjoys complications and subtlety, then a fountain pen is not for you."

A pit.

His own.

A life in ruins, he thinks.

X

hen you think of fire," Joe asked Parsifal one day, "what comes into your mind?"

"Warmth," Parsifal said. "Light. Small birds roasting on a spit. Flame. Burning logs (does that count?). Orange. Screams. Red. Ouch. Mother. Why do you want to know?"

Joe lifted a paperweight from his desk, tossed it into the air, and caught it several times. It was nothing more than a black stone—a piece of lava or something—but the therapist seemed to find it comforting because he kept on playing with it.

Then Joe picked up his yellow legal pad and wrote something down. He got up. "Excuse me," he said, "I need to use the bathroom."

Joe left, taking the pad with him, his sandals slapping the floor on his way to the bathroom in the hall outside his office. Parsifal knew that bathroom well. It was squalid, with a hand dryer that only put out cold air. It had a dirty sink and a stall with a door that wouldn't close, the inside of which had been covered with various violent and incomprehensibly threatening messages left, he assumed, by Joe's other clients—not a good lot, all in all. Parsifal got up and hefted the stone in his hand. It didn't feel special. It didn't feel like anything but a stone.

After a surprisingly long time, Joe returned. "What was it you were asking?" he said.

"I wanted to know why you asked me about fire?"

"Oh," Joe said. "For no particular reason." He picked up the stone and put it down again. "Maybe I was feeling chilly."

What is this fear that falls into my heart?

The body Parsifal had discovered in the pit he had dug to catch a deer was of a man, and clearly the stranger had died instantly, face down, impaled on the spikes Parsifal had wedged into the ground a few days before. The severity of the impact had been no doubt increased by the weight of a large sack of brown rice the man had been carrying when he had fallen, and the spikes had run straight through the stranger's chest. The stranger was wearing a dark suit and a baseball hat, which, oddly, had remained on his head, even as the rice scattered all around his body. Because many of the grains were covered with the man's blood, they gave the appearance of the red sprinkles on the tops of the cupcakes that Conrad used to bring him, as a special treat, once in a while. Someone, either the man or some other person, had tied several bags around the dead man's waist, and these were also stained by blood, and worse.

What would Pearl say? Parsifal wondered. He was only fourteen, not quite grown, and Conrad was gone, as usual, so wasn't around to give any advice on the matter. As a result, Parsifal acted out of instinct as much as anything. First, he knew enough that for him to touch the body would only leave behind a trail of evidence that might confuse anyone who ventured this far into the forest to search for the man. The last thing he needed, then or ever, was a prison term. Second, the man was clearly dead, and his grave had already been dug, so to speak. That would have been the hard part, anyway, so all Parsifal needed to do was to fill it in with the dirt he had pushed to one side earlier when he had dug the hole, and then afterward to cover that with a layer of leaves and tamp it down so that only an eye trained in woodcraft would be able to detect any irregularity. In a month not even an expert would know what lay

Moss, yes. The cold wetness of his shoes in a stream, yes again, but it was the wetness of no particular stream that he could identify. He decided that later, when he took the blindfold off, he would change his socks.

His ankle began to throb.

Above him, Parsifal heard a sound from the sky, a flapping of wings, or a hum, as if something was continuing to follow his erratic progress through the forest, and in the midst of everything else, the sound seemed a comfort. In a way it felt comforting even though—or perhaps *because*—he couldn't actually see a thing through the blindfold. Was it growing dark? He couldn't tell, but at the rate he was moving, propelled by those energy bars, he didn't see why he needed to stop at all, let alone for darkness. Whether the result of ge-nius or terror, Parsifal could feel himself going up hills, crawling on his hands and knees like a powerful baby, and descending them upright, his back leaning into the pull of gravity, the heels of his soggy boots digging into the earth, his cane striking grass, leaves, and wood.

Then, through the humming/flapping above him, he detected yet another sound, one so faint that he was sure he would not have noticed it if he had been dis-tracted by the world of sight. The sound grew louder and, without hesitating for a moment, Parsifal whipped off the blindfold, blinking at the sky just in time to see an Airstream trailer heading straight at him. Quickly he leaped to one side, and as he did the trailer came crashing down right where he had been standing. He looked around. It wasn't nearly as late in the day as he had guessed, only about two in the afternoon, by his watch.

Parsifal stood, his limbs aflutter, and sat down again. Then, still shaking, he rose to his wet feet again and gathered a few dry branches to start a fire to make tea. Upon reflection, the blindness experiment had been a failure, even though it had allowed him to hear the Airstream more easily and may have saved his life. Still, in the long run he could not tell much difference between searching with or without sight, except for the extra bruises. Neither had brought him measurably closer to his goal.

Parsifal sipped his tea, and for the first time forced himself to stare at what was left of the fallen trailer, now only a shiny foil packet of aluminum, about twelve feet by six feet by six inches. The impact had crushed the doors, as well as a bumper that proclaimed, *We're Spending Our Kids' College Fund.*

Parsifal had often heard of the awesome power of tornados regarding trailers and trailer parks, but had never actually witnessed it in person. Had anyone been living inside when the Airstream was carried into the sky? It was possible, but if so, there could have been no survivors. "Rest in peace," he whispered, and then, overcome by the desire to rest himself, spread out his sleeping bag, changed his wet socks, and, even though it was still early in the day, fell immediately to sleep.

In his dream he was blind. Nothing fancy, just the conventional sort of blindness—straight black, without a speck of light anywhere, not even gray. And no matter what he did (it wasn't much), the blindness would not disappear or fade, even for a moment. But at least he wasn't dead.

Rest in peace, stranger in the pit.

Rest in peace, old couple possibly still inside the Airstream.

Parsifal thought about the suit the dead man in the pit had been wearing. Except for his father, it was unusual for anyone to wear such formal attire in the forest. It was entirely possible, he surmised, that the dead man may have been a fellow stockbroker of Conrad's who had offered to take Pearl and Parsifal a sack of rice, Conrad being tied up at that moment with a big deal.

Sometimes, as a child, lying awake at night in the forest, Parsifal heard the screams of wild cats, the short, choked cries of dying things, the silent scuffle of somebody's pet dog running down a desperate deer. Then everything grew quiet except for Pearl's heavy breathing and the rustle of wind through leaves.

How well Parsifal remembers those evenings when, after a long absence, he would hear the sounds of his father's arrival: first Parsifal heard the sounds of snapping twigs and muttered curses, then his father's familiar tread along the path that led to their house, then the knock on their door, and when Parsifal pushed it open, there was Conrad, carrying whatever surprises he'd brought with him.

"Hello, young man," Conrad said, and shook his son's hand (he used to joke that too much intimacy spoiled a child). Next, after carefully hanging his jacket on a coat hanger Parsifal had made from branches, Conrad washed his face and hands and waited for Pearl to bring supper to the stump that served as the family's rustic table. His father, Parsifal remembers, liked to pass the time until dinner was served squashing insects with his thumb.

Then the family ate, and afterward Conrad stood behind Pearl as she washed the dishes, rubbing her

back and shoulders in silent communication to show
how much he had missed her. When Pearl finished the
dishes, Conrad returned to his chair at the stump and
Pearl took out the comb she kept in the breadbox, running it through Conrad's hair again and again, alter-
nately covering and uncovering the bald spot he was
just beginning to exhibit, but which he usually kept
covered with a baseball cap.

After that the two of them would send Parsifal out
on some errand, and when he returned an hour or two
later, Conrad was in bed fast asleep, alongside Parsifal's
mother, of course.

On three-day weekends, or weekends when Conrad
was able to spend more time with his family, he and
Parsifal often took long walks, during which Conrad
explained the principles of hedge funds, or discussed
the pros and cons of high executive compensation.
Sometimes Conrad interrupted these lessons to tell
Parsifal that he had no idea how lucky he was to escape
the pettiness and competition of what most people
might have called "a normal education."

"They are nothing more than frightened apes,
Parsifal," Conrad told him, "students and teachers
alike." Then he rubbed Parsifal's head in an affectionate
manner, and the two of them returned for supper. In no
time, his father left once again for the city.

Frightened, murderous apes.

Parsifal ate another energy bar and stared at the flattened Airstream. It was morning, but whatever amiable oldsters had been trapped inside would never see it, the only compensation perhaps—their spending spree having been halted by the power of the air—that their children and grandchildren would now be able to attend the universities of their choice. For the first time Parsifal noticed lying next to the trailer a small shovel, like a foxhole tool, that must have been strapped to the trailer's side. He walked over and picked it up. It had not been damaged at all.

What should Parsifal do next? The advantage of trying out the blindfold was that at least it had been a *plan*. Now he had nowhere to point himself toward in search of the cup, no clue as to what to do next. Parsifal sat there, feeling the powerful energy of Misty's bar surge through him. Off in the distance he was fairly sure that he could just make out the sounds of "Rainy Day Women." He rose, and the voices stopped. In their place he could hear that same humming/flapping sound he had heard earlier, but the morning fog made it impossible to see exactly from where it originated. Parsifal strained to listen.

On the one hand, humming and flapping, and on the other, the words of the rock and roll classic.

He tied the shovel to his backpack, then heaved the pack onto his shoulders.

$$M + C + BD + P - (C + BD) = M + P$$

Parsifal walked in what he guessed was the direction of the voices but found nothing, so he kept walking. At least, he thought, it was a direction. A light rain began to fall, which turned to a medium rain, then to an actual downpour. The good thing about the rain wasn't just that it helped things grow, but that for one reason or another, very few objects ever fell out of the sky while it was raining. He'd heard a dozen discussions on radio talk shows about why this should be the case, but out of all of them he'd never heard a completely convincing answer.

At last it was time to quit for the day. Parsifal looked around for a place that would be dry (they weren't as hard to find in the forest as many people might think), and almost immediately spotted a cave just a few yards away, its entrance marked by a few wet, insubstantial bushes. It wasn't tall enough for a man to stand up in it—though maybe a child could—but the low arch of its opening provided sufficient room for anyone to stretch out in relative comfort. Parsifal crouched inside beneath the gentle dome of its entrance. It went back only a few yards, but it was dry, with a clean, sandy floor. There was even a pile of dry twigs off to one side that he could use to start a fire. He backed out and quickly gathered several larger wet logs for later in the evening (it was the afternoon by then) and for the night. He carried them inside.

Parsifal started his fire near the entrance so the smoke would blow outside, took off his socks, pulled on a fresh pair, and propped the worn ones up near the fire with a stick. Despite his clean socks, he realized that he was cold and far more weary than he'd guessed. He rolled out his sleeping bag and crawled inside of it.

A nap would feel good, he thought, *and if by any chance I sleep through the night, so much the better*.

Parsifal lay his head down and struck something really hard. He shook his head. He must have been tired, because he had just ignored one of the very first rules of woodcraft: always check the ground where you are about to sleep to be sure there are no hidden rocks or roots. He raised himself up and felt beneath where his head had been. His hand touched something smooth, like metal. Parsifal dug around a little more—it wasn't buried very deep—and pulled it out. It *was* metal.

It was an old, ornate brass doorknob, without a hole to insert a key, but with a pattern of leaves forming an oval around its flat surface. Parsifal couldn't imagine what a doorknob would be doing there without a door unless some creature, a porcupine or beaver, had dragged the whole door there, to what must have been its den, and then eaten the wood, leaving behind the knob like a bone. But on second thought, the door would have been far too heavy for a porcupine, even a strong one, to pull along behind it. The doorknob looked familiar. It looked familiar because, he saw, it was the doorknob to his old house, once so important to him, lost, found, hidden, and now found again, and though it was far too late to bring back Pearl or to allow Conrad to return to his family once again, it was undeniably *his*.

It must be a sign, Parsifal thought, and put it in his pocket.

Three white anchors on a field of green.

XI

he next morning was sunny, and Parsifal was greeted almost immediately upon waking by the spectacle of about a thousand polyethylene cutting boards flip-flopping their way like bright white playing cards down from a cloudless sky. Not to say they couldn't be deadly if one caught a person with its edge, but protected by the entrance of the cave he was able to simply eat an energy bar and enjoy the sight of them. Parsifal considered picking up a small one that had a handle (they came in assorted sizes), to take back with him, but he didn't want to lose the focus of his search, and besides, he already was carrying the shovel. Another time, he told himself. The cutting boards were indestructible. They would be there for him if he ever returned.

"You know," Joe said to Parsifal one Saturday morning, as Parsifal was making up for a session he'd missed the previous week when he accidentally had been researching one thing or another in the library straight through the time for his appointment, "I wouldn't be surprised if you didn't harbor a lot of resentment over the fact that your childhood was basically taken away from you by having to survive in a harsh environment without a single friend. I can imagine the anger you must have felt seeing those contented children at the Happy Bunny. It must have created an enormous desire in your subconscious to destroy the pleasure of those preschoolers, just as your own potentially normal childhood had been withheld from you during your difficult life in the forest. Does that strike a note, Parsifal?"

Joe sipped coffee from a large paper cup and every so often took another bite from what was left of a bag of jelly donuts he had lying on his desk. He had offered Parsifal one earlier, but Parsifal had refused. Joe had called the donuts his "breakfast," in what Parsifal suspected was an attempt to make him feel guilty for having missed his appointment a week earlier. For once, Joe's casual attire had seemed appropriate, and Parsifal watched as the increasingly overweight therapist wiped a corner of his mouth with the smooth paper the donuts came wrapped in. Then Joe rubbed the big toe of his left foot with the bottom of the sandal on his right one. Parsifal didn't mind his sloppiness, considering it was the weekend, but he did find it somewhat insulting that the man hadn't bothered to shave. Where were his professional standards?

"Are you growing a beard?" Parsifal asked.

Joe wrote something down on his yellow pad. Parsifal could see that whatever it was, Joe had underlined part of it twice.

"Why do you ask that?" Joe said. "Did my previous question make you uncomfortable? Did your father have a beard?"

"Well, you *haven't* shaved," Parsifal answered, "and actually my father never had the slightest bit of facial hair."

Joe paused to write something else. "I'm relieved to hear you say that," he said. "But I was thinking that you seem to be in some denial concerning the unpleasant reality of your early years in the woods. For example, it might not be a bad idea to try to relive them, and by that I don't mean you'd have to redo the entire time, minute by minute, but if, for example, you were able to hold on to one single thing—by which I mean an object—no matter how small or insignificant it might be, that you associate with your life back in the forest, even a fork or knife or cup—you people did have utensils, didn't you?—something like that might go a long way toward bringing back up to the surface the massive sense of resentment you are currently repressing. What do you think about that? And then, of course, there's the scar."

"It's possible," Parsifal had said. "I'll have to give it some more thought."

At social gatherings, complete strangers, when they find out what Parsifal does for a living, often come up to him and say, "Parsifal, is there anything really out-of-the-box funny you can think of that happened concerning fountain pens? If so, I'd like to hear it."

Actually, that is not as difficult a question to answer as you might think, because while pens, especially fountain pens, aren't exactly known for provoking levity, Parsifal does have a story he enjoys telling: Once, when he happened to be standing in court on trial for arson, and the prosecutor was making his closing argument before the judge, becoming more and more outraged every minute over the supposedly terrible things he claimed Parsifal had done and of which Parsifal knew himself to be innocent, the prosecutor, because he was starting to work up a sweat, took off his sport coat.

But what the man didn't realize was that with the jacket off, everyone—that is, the judge, Parsifal, Walter, and a whole gallery of curious onlookers—could see that the fountain pen in the man's shirt pocket had managed to detach itself from its top, which was still clipped there, so that the ink from the body of the pen was running out onto the front of his shirt. The longer the prosecutor talked and the angrier he became—it was impossible to tell if the man was sincere or if he was making it up—the larger the stain on his shirt got. "I could see that the bailiff was beginning to smile," Parsifal adds, "because he probably was wondering, as I was, if the stain would reach all the way to the guy's belt before he finished."

It didn't, and Parsifal concludes his story by telling how his attorney, Walter, had a good chuckle. "You can thank that stain for getting you off," he told Parsifal when he took him to lunch following the verdict. "I should buy that guy a whole box of pens and see if he'll use them at every trial."

This was before Parsifal got into the business.

When Parsifal first came to the city, he began to know people in the following way: he would find a popular event—a theater opening or a sporting match or even a movie—and join the long line to buy tickets. While he was in the line, he listened quietly to the conversations around him. Sometimes he would let people cut in ahead of him, telling them he was waiting for some friends to arrive. No one bothered him or asked him any questions. Then, when he finally reached the ticket window, he would pretend he had forgotten something—usually his wallet—or that he had left a pan heating on the stove, and leave. "I'd hate to have my house burn down," he'd tell the person standing in line behind him.

In this way he furthered his education in the ways of city people and gained knowledge that served him well in those weeks before he discovered how helpful librarians could be.

The sky had cleared to a brilliant blue, but there was no trace of the bird that had been overhead.

What does it mean to be blind? It means not to see, of course. That time, in the crawl space beneath the Happy Bunny it was cold and dark, and the only way to see and to keep warm at the same time was to set a fire.

Parsifal walked. He listened. He felt the stone rub against the doorknob in his pocket, but he did not hear either Misty or her friends.

What is this obsession with blindness that creeps into the heart?

It was only a few days after his encounter with the first blind man that Parsifal met another one. This second blind man was very tall and elegantly dressed, and standing at a stoplight listening—Parsifal understands now—for the sound of traffic to die away so he could cross the street. This blind man had neither a guide dog nor a white cane, and the only thing that might have indicated his disability was the pair of dark glasses that Parsifal believed at first was there simply to protect the man's eyes from the sun, for in those days he knew little about blindness.

"Excuse me," Parsifal asked him, "have you by any chance seen my father?" He then began to describe Conrad, and the more he did, the more the man began to chuckle, until at the end, when Parsifal got to the part about how Conrad was upset by certain shades of yellow—not all of them, he explained—the man was holding his stomach and laughing so hard that various passersby slowed their pace to look at the two of them.

Then the man said, "My son, I haven't seen anything for over twenty years, ever since, as a young man of about your age—if I judge the sound of your voice correctly—I wasn't paying attention to where I was going and stepped straight into a pit dug by a crew working on some pipes that ran under the sidewalk. I hit my head on a plank and woke up in the hospital, unable to see. So I hope you will excuse me if I'm having a laugh at this moment, even if it's at my own expense, over the fact that you're asking me if I have seen your father. Ha, ha, ha, ha."

Parsifal thanked him, and soon afterward he stopped asking that question of strangers.

How many days had Parsifal been in the forest? Two? Three? Four? Time was doing funny things, and he was beginning to lose track, but honestly, that didn't bother him. According to *The Old Trapper's Guide to Wood-Craft*, one of the secrets of survival was to change from "city time" to what it called "wild time." Accordingly, Parsifal came to the resolution that he would go on searching for Fenjewla as long as he possibly could, but if he had to stop before he achieved his goal, that was all right too, because he would return to the city knowing he had done all that he was able.

For that matter, he could always return and try again later, and maybe bring a compass and a metal detector the next time, so that leaving the forest on this trip without finding Fenjewla would not really bother him all that much. What *did* bother him—troubled him, he supposed, like something that had been resting in the back of his mind the whole time he was in the forest, walking and sleeping and zigzagging and whatnot—was that not once had he ever actually encountered one of the forest's edges—some place where the trees ended and a person could look out and see a distant steeple, or peer through a screen of blackberry bushes at a family in their backyard as they prepared their barbecue.

It wasn't a huge deal, but as he said, this thought regarding the forest's absence of boundaries was pretty much there in some form every minute.

Along with the panic.

Along with Misty.

The last time Parsifal saw Joe, Joe was wearing what Parsifal believed were called "cargo shorts"—shorts, in any case, with lots of pockets—and a yellow Hawaiian shirt with purple parrots and green palm trees.

"You know," he said as soon as Parsifal sat down, "you've come a long way from the mess you were when I first began seeing you, and I must say I've enjoyed our conversations. It's seldom I find a patient so unusual, so stimulating, so able to dredge up details of a past as unique as yours. That's why I'm feeling sad to tell you I think it's time we called it quits, not only because the funds for your treatment allotted to me by the state have run out, but also because over the past few sessions"—and here he consulted his yellow pad—"this transference thing seems to be getting a whole lot stronger."

Parsifal, totally unprepared for what he'd just heard, remained temporarily frozen, and could only stare at the picture hanging on the wall of Joe's office, one he'd never really looked at before. It depicted a room in one of those early, primitive mental-health institutions in which several lightly clad female patients were being sprayed by fire hoses directed by brutal attendants. The women looked justifiably angry, even as the thinness of their garments, clinging as they were to their lush bodies, made them, if anything, more attractive than ever.

"Once again, I repeat, I don't exactly see how that could be the case," Parsifal answered, "because at least insofar as your respective styles of dressing are concerned, you and my father are complete opposites. You are casual to the point of being slovenly, while my father was formal to the point of being fastidious. As a person you are open and interested in long conversations centered around my feelings, while my father wanted to hear nothing about how I felt, but took pride only in teaching me the principles of bookkeeping. Your face is hairy and my father's was smooth-shaven. My father, for all of the sedentary work he did in the city, managed to stay in remarkably good physical shape, and was capable of carrying over his shoulder for miles a heavy sack of peanuts or dried beans, not to mention bags of extra stuff tied to his belt at his waist. In your case, while I understand that criminal psychiatry is pretty much of a sedentary occupation, you appear to have succumbed to it completely and, considering your diet, which seems to be mostly coffee, donuts, and Chinese takeout, I'd say it's remarkable that you're alive at all."

Joe wrote a line or two on his pad. "It seems to me I'm detecting some hostility here. I understand where you are coming from, Parsifal. And without years of intense psychological study most people would find it nearly impossible to believe that it is in precisely such cases, where the psyche is able to trick itself into believing that there is no connection whatsoever, that the transference issue I am speaking of most easily takes place."

Parsifal doubted Joe was right, but what choice did he have? Parsifal knew it was Joe's right, as his therapist, to terminate their relationship, just as any parent can leave a child behind whenever he wishes. Parsifal was very sorry, of course, but that was that. He shut the door behind him, walked outside, and stepped over the beginnings of a small sinkhole that had begun to form at the foot of the stairs and that was probably caused by a leaking water pipe.

It was the last time Parsifal was to see Joe alive because, in what was an amazing coincidence, the following week when Joe left his office one night, the deficient-in-night-vision therapist stepped straight into a pit someone must have dug in front of the steps. Whoever *they* were—plumbers or construction workers—and whoever *they* had been sent by—Joe's landlord (who claimed to know nothing) or the city—the men had left behind in the bottom of the pit several sharpened copper pipes that had been pushed into the earth so they were sticking straight into the air, one of which went right through Joe's heart when he toppled onto it, still holding a bag of corn chips, completely unaware that the pit must have been dug while he had been inside his office, filling out Medicare forms or court papers, or doing whatever.

Parsifal felt sad, naturally, but couldn't help wonder whether Joe might still be alive if he had not terminated their relationship prematurely, because if Joe had not, then Parsifal surely would have been able to warn him about those plumbers when he arrived for his appointment on that fateful night. Or possibly, if Joe had prolonged their conversation—something Joe claimed

to enjoy while at the same time enforcing the limita-
tions of what he called "the therapeutic hour"—and
talked with Parsifal for just a short while longer, by
then those plumbers would have returned and covered
their dangerous pit with boards. Or at least removed
those pipes.

Parsifal guessed that no one would ever know the
answer to this for sure.

So Parsifal moved through the forest. Curiously, the
result of having worn a blindfold for a while, and then
not, was to see the world through different eyes (was his
vision starting to blur?). Parsifal saw a colony of gigantic fungi in the shape of human hearts, red, fist-sized,
and pulpy, throbbing in the leaf-filtered light. He saw a
huge tree he could not name, but which was laden with
small fruit, the size of figs, clearly rotting where they
hung, refusing to drop. Instead, each liquefied from
within, and at the bottom of each fruit its moisture collected into a single drop until, with a gentle plop, it fell
to the barren ground around the tree. Parsifal walked
up and touched the liquid at the tip of one of those
fruits with his finger and put it to his mouth. It was not
sweet, as he had expected, but salty.

Parsifal passed dejected willow trees, encountered a
clump of bushes that hung their fuzzy heads in shame,

strolled by a stand of agoraphobic alders, looked out over a small pond covered with a layer of hallucinated scum, climbed a low, repressed hill, kicked up a troubled patch of moss, passed beneath an anxious sycamore, a bulimic waterfall, an obsessive nest of wasps, a panicked porcupine, more than one repressed log, a paranoidal swamp, a narcissistic . . . well . . . narcissus, walked beneath a passive-aggressive set of overhanging branches, over an enabling path, through several patches of toxic poison oak, near a manic maple, and beneath a neurotic nuthatch fixated on something on a distant branch.

Was there a message here?

Probably. And if only Joe had kept him on as a patient, he might have been around to answer it.

Parsifal walked on.

Sometimes when Parsifal had a fever, Pearl would lay clumps of damp moss on his forehead and, if the fever was severe, also in his armpits and on his groin. The moss felt cool, and later, when it had absorbed his body's heat, Pearl would return it to whatever place she had taken it from.

"For the next time," she used to say.

And: "A person has to plan ahead."

Not very surprisingly, not a single one of those plumbers, whoever they were, who had been responsible for Joe's fatal accident ever stepped forward to admit his honest error.

Parsifal had not gone much farther in the forest when, putting his foot down into a small depression, he found it deeper than he'd judged and twisted his ankle. It hurt, so he took off his sock to look at it. The ankle was swollen and had already begun to change color, so he laced his boot slightly tighter to give it more support, and cut himself a new cane to use in walking. Somehow he must have left the last one behind when he removed the blindfold. He also took the time to change into a dry pair of socks. Then he ate half an energy bar, which took the pain away, and he began to travel again, but slowly. He had had enough. He resolved that the very second he came to the end of the forest, he would take the next bus home. Forget following the creek to the sea. Forget the door. Forget about Fenjewla—at least for now. He had made a reasonable try; there was no point in endangering his health over the matter.

Misty.

Above him, though the sky was clear, Parsifal still saw no sign of that persistent bird, or plane, or whatever it may have been.

Was he sorry to see it gone?

Almost.

When Parsifal was small enough that Pearl could hold him in her lap, they would sit waiting for Conrad to arrive home from the city where he had been staying in his comfortable but—he took pains to assure them—modest townhouse. While the two waited, Pearl sat on a swing made out of a log and two thick vines, and rocked quietly, holding Parsifal. Sometimes she sang, smelling all the while of fresh leaves and the flowers she had tucked into her hair to please Conrad, and Parsifal would fall asleep.

Of all the time he spent in the forest, this was his favorite.

The silence of a falling star

Once Pearl and Parsifal waited a whole month for Conrad to arrive with the antibiotics to treat a disease Pearl told Parsifal his father had accidentally passed on to her.

Lights up the purple sky

Pearl said that she held no grudges, and sometimes that was the price a man had to pay for having a secretary.

Fenjewla.

XII

fountain pen forces no one to read its words.

A pen writes only as necessary, running out of ink every so often to remind a person he or she is mortal, and also to give the writer a little extra time to think about what to say next.

A pen does not censor the content of its writing.

A pen does not even need to use words but can write symbols and draw pictures.

A fountain pen needs no batteries.

A pen does not have to be plugged in and charged.

A fountain pen, no matter how beautiful it is, will lie humbly in a drawer until it is wanted.

A fountain pen, with just a little rinse now and again, will never need replacing, except for a new sac or piston seal every so often in the course of normal use, an easy enough job for a trusted person who repairs fountain pens.

The writing produced by a pen not only provides words but also gives insight into the character of the writer.

Treated carefully, a fountain pen will last for a long, long time.

Parsifal's ankle was starting to hurt even more.

Sometimes he wondered if his mother could have been blind, because how else to explain her sending Parsifal out to find food while she stayed back in their small house made of branches, "tidying up"? How else to explain that when there were leaks and the rain or snow came inside, Pearl would have to wait for Conrad to return from the city or, when Parsifal was older, to have him climb up on the roof and repair the places where water got in? How else to explain the lack of mirrors, and Pearl's reluctance to go far from the house (with the one disastrous exception of her following him out at the time of the forest fire) unless she was in the company of Conrad, and the fact that when Conrad would arrive from the city, carrying a sack of whole wheat, or chickpeas, or couscous, Pearl would tell Parsifal, "I hear your father coming," and never say, "I see your father"?

Because yes, now that Parsifal was back in the same forest in which he was raised, it all was starting to fall into place, despite the warning Joe would have given him had he lived: the fact was that for him—as for any child—the world he was born into seemed the normal one, the one by which all others were measured. Therefore it was no wonder that when Parsifal saw his first blind man in the city he did not know what to make of him. No wonder that the man seemed no different from anyone else, and especially no different from Pearl. No wonder Pearl had never taken a trip to the city to track Conrad down to see how he *really* spent his life there, had never gone on her own to the pharmacy to buy the antibiotics she had such need of, or ever tracked down Margot, her husband's secretary, to give her a piece of her mind and maybe punch her. No wonder Pearl had never even visited the townhouse where Conrad stayed, but instead accepted his poor excuse that it wasn't clean enough for her because his housekeeper had stopped coming. No wonder Pearl had chosen to stay there, in the forest, apart from most people, and to live out the only life she knew. Thus it was, when the fire raged behind her, Pearl had sent Parsifal away to safety on the outside rather than risk a life where she would be pitied.

Yes, Parsifal thought: *Pearl must have been blind.* That would explain why Conrad had carved those anchors in the tree by their front door—not, as Conrad had claimed, because his family were the anchors in his life—but so that by running her small hands over the tree's rough bark, Pearl could find the mark on that one tree out of all the other ones in the forest, the mark that would tell her she was home.

It felt as if Parsifal suddenly understood everything: the forest, his isolation as a child, his mother's often messed-up though always beautiful appearance, plus the fact that Pearl never wore makeup, something Parsifal had earlier attributed to what Pearl had called "the natural look." His mother had been *blind*, but *Parsifal* had been the one all these years who had not seen, and now that he did, what a difference it made.

No wonder she had burned to death in the fire.

Parsifal walked on, the ache in his ankle growing worse.

And then, there he was, sitting with his back against an ancient oak, eating the last half of his last energy bar (it made the pain go away), when a shower of silver paper clips darkened the sky. Even falling from a great height, they weren't heavy enough to do serious harm, so Parsifal stayed where he was and simply raised his backpack above his head to protect himself until the storm had passed.

Parsifal was fine, and there appeared to be no major damage to the forest except that a few leaves had gotten sliced up pretty badly. But paper clips? He wondered. He no longer believed the sky would ever run out of ammunition—and this *was* disturbing. But suppose instead that the clips were intended as a kind of warning, like those pamphlets dropped by the US Air Force over Nagasaki. (Did we drop pamphlets? Parsifal was pretty certain we did not, but he couldn't remember for sure, and, actually, thinking about it, Nagasaki was kind of an afterthought, with no warning at all, like the story of someone who is cold and, looking around for something to make into a small fire, finds a few milk cartons and old coloring books that he might burn to keep him warm.)

During Parsifal's early days of therapy, Joe confided to him that before becoming a therapist, but after his days in the army, he had worked for several years as a stockbroker, rising to near the top of his profession. But the pressure had gotten to him, Joe said, and that was probably the explanation for his present slovenly attire. "I may have overdone the casual part as a reaction to all my years in the business world, where snappy dressing is de rigueur," he added, kicking off his sandals and wiggling his fat, hairy toes as if to demonstrate his freedom.

"Oh," Parsifal said, "then maybe you knew my father. He was a well-known stockbroker, too." He told Joe his name was Conrad.

Joe thought for a bit, and then wrote something down on his yellow pad.

"As a matter of fact," Joe answered, "I've never known anyone at all whose name was Conrad."

And then—assuming that his field of vision was like the screen of a television set (albeit one that needed adjusting)—from the right of the TV screen, out of view behind a stand of maples on the other side of the broad meadow that stretched out before him, Parsifal could once again hear the sounds of voices singing—no, chanting—although they were too far away to make out the actual words. He listened as the sound moved slowly across the hypothetical screen, still behind the meadow, but now obscured by a stand of sycamores, the sign of riparian woodland, the trees indicating that there was probably a source of water, maybe even a creek, nearby.

He sat still and listened. The chanting sounded like "Give me a dollar," but he couldn't be certain, muffled as it was by leaves and branches. Then, as if the group— it *had* to be Misty, Cody, and Black Dog—had come upon a gigantic catapult abandoned in the wilderness and suddenly they had shot themselves all the way to the left of the television screen, the chanting, without ever having passed through the center, now came from behind a scraggly group of oaks on the formerly silent left side and had reverted once again to the unintelligible.

"Wait," Parsifal called out, but even as he did, he knew in his weakened condition that his voice would not carry that distance. He rose and began to hobble quickly toward them. *It's just possible that I can negotiate a couple more energy bars to tide me over until I can find my way out of here,* he thought. *But my ankle hurts too much for the long haul.*

Then, as the sound disappeared altogether, Parsifal sat there, leaning on his cane and gasping, and the television screen went blank.

Pain.

Parsifal lay on his back, looking up at the sky and breathing through his mouth, when a shadow blocked the sun.

"Look everyone," Misty said, "the Pen Man is still here."

Cody walked closer and poked Parsifal with his foot. He groaned and opened his eyes.

"He's alive," Cody said. He seemed neither happy nor particularly unhappy about that fact.

Black Dog, however, sat a few feet away in a kind of Indian squat, and kept his face hidden in his hands. "This is so bad," Black Dog said. "This is such a bummer." He was wearing the same leather pants as when Parsifal had first seen him, and they certainly were not improved by their use.

Cody took Parsifal's pulse and unstrapped Parsifal's wristwatch. It was operated by a quartz battery and kept really good time. Cody put it in his pocket. "His pulse is pretty good," Cody said.

Parsifal should have complained, but he seemed to be thinking of something far away that he could not quite name at the moment.

"Shit," Misty said. "What are we going to do?"

In Parsifal's opinion, Misty had never looked better. Maybe it was the fresh air, maybe the three were on some sort of fast and purification thing, he didn't know, but her cheeks were red and her eyes sparkled. God forbid it could have been the results of group sex. But on the other hand, Cody and Black Dog seemed not in the least better for wear, so maybe that was not the case. Misty was a woman who never needed to apply makeup, Parsifal thought.

Then he felt something strange at his hips. It turned out to be Cody, who was going through his pockets. Was Cody looking for a health insurance card? Parsifal doubted it, and besides, he didn't have one. Cody finished, and stuffed everything back and gave Parsifal a sort of farewell poke with his foot.

"Well," Black Dog said. He said it very slowly, and it seemed to last a long time. He began to chant, "Give me a dollar, give me a dollar," but Parsifal couldn't make any more sense of it then than the first time he'd heard it. Still, it seemed to settle Black Dog down.

Misty sat cross-legged by Parsifal's head and stared at him. "Not so fast," she said. "We have to think this through."

There was silence, and no one moved.

"If we try to carry him out of here there may by trouble." She looked hard at Cody. "But if we just leave him here, there's a good chance he may die."

"Give me a dollar," Black Dog said.

"On the other hand," Parsifal heard Misty continue, "karmically speaking, it doesn't make any difference at all whatever we choose to do, because Pen Man's fate has already been predetermined by his own actions, and what is dying anyway besides simply moving to another plane of existence?"

Cody began to unlace Parsifal's boots.

"Stop," Misty said. "You want to have people looking around afterward to try to figure out what happened?"

"So," Cody said.

"So let's get out of here," Misty said.

Black Dog stood up and Cody shrugged.

"Oh, and Cody . . ."

Cody waited for Misty to finish.

"Put the watch back."

In the distance Parsifal heard that strange chant, *Give me a dollar*, grow fainter.

All voices the same voice.

All requests the same request.

Was this a dream, or did it really happen?

When Parsifal regained consciousness he had his watch and his boots were still laced, but by the time he remembered to look for footprints he had traveled too far to turn around and go back, even considering the fact that technically he didn't know if he was going back or forward, and his ankle hurt a lot.

And the doorknob was missing.

His infinite wisdom.

All birds circling overhead the same bird.

Actually, his ankle was killing him.

XIII

or the record: it *wasn't* that Parsifal *hadn't* felt really bad for all those children whose lives had been destroyed, or at least substantially altered, by the fire at the Happy Bunny. He *had*, but he *hadn't* started the fire as part of some master plan to destroy every preschooler in sight. It wasn't as if he had some secret agenda that involved burning down preschools, at least not one that anyone had discovered (just joking!). After the court released him, Parsifal wasn't going to go straight to the nearest toddler farm and burn it down. Contrary to Joe's crafty intimations, he wasn't angry in the least. It was only that he *had* been cold, and wanted to get warm—a basic human desire, right?

"What good," Walter had asked the judge, "would it do to punish this pathetic specimen of parental neglect further?" True or not, it was enough to convince the court. Nor, for the record, *had* Parsifal so much as tossed a candy wrapper into the play yard of any preschool he had walked by (and there had been a lot of them) since then.

Parsifal unfastened the laces on his boot in order to examine his ankle. Actually, his whole foot was a yellow-blue-black color, and the throbbing had moved to his knee. There was no question of continuing his search; this was serious. Parsifal had to exit the forest, for sure. The only trouble was that he didn't know exactly how. All he could think was to abandon that whole zigzag strategy and just continue walking in a straight line. It didn't really matter what direction he chose; sooner or later (sooner, if he was lucky) he had to emerge onto that backyard barbecue scene he'd imagined earlier: the dad in an apron, the mom and the kids holding out their plates. "Hey," they would say, "you don't look so good. Why don't you take a minute to have a burger and then we'll give you a ride to the ER? Rare or medium? How about it? What do you say?"

But it hurt to walk—a lot—and every small tuft of grass, every pebble was excruciating. Parsifal didn't know what Cody had done to his watch, but it had stopped working, so he couldn't tell how long he'd actually lain there, and now it was starting to grow dark. *One more night*, Parsifal told himself, *hang on, and after a little stop at the emergency room to have your ankle looked at and your fluid balance restored, should that be necessary, you will be back home with your friends and your writing implements.*

What friends?

Not far ahead he spotted another small cliff—a ledge, really—no more than three feet high, but it had been dug out in such a way that created a sort of break from the wind. It wasn't perfect, but there wasn't a cave around, and he wasn't going to hobble about in search of one. Also, the cliff was near a good supply of wood to use for a fire. The wood was oak, dry, and the pieces were large enough to burn all night. He pulled together a stack of leaves to make a mattress for his sleeping bag, fixing it so the end with his hurt leg would be slightly higher than its companion. He fished around in his pocket for some matches to start a fire, but to his surprise, they were gone. Parsifal checked again, and went through all his pockets. Had they fallen out somewhere? They must have, or Cody had taken them. The only thing at all that he could find was the stone Black Dog had left behind, and he didn't even know why he was still carrying it with him.

The sound of owl wings.

The next morning Parsifal's whole leg felt like a solid piece of wood—not just the ankle but his entire leg— but wood that could somehow feel pain, and wood that had swollen up during the night despite its having been elevated. The only way he could move was by digging his cane into the soft earth and then pulling his bad leg after it. After an hour of this, he could still look back and see the place where he had spent the night.

He needed to get lucky, and fast.

Joe's was the first memorial service Parsifal had ever attended, and why he had chosen to go was hard for him to say. Maybe it was to see if any of Joe's former stockbroker colleagues might be there—people who might have known Conrad, whom Parsifal couldn't help but think Joe had known, but hadn't wanted to tell him about, because to do so would have compromised Joe's stringent code of professional ethics. Certainly, Joe had a strange look on his face when he'd told Parsifal he hadn't known his father. Or maybe Parsifal came to the memorial only because Joe had been the receptacle for more information about his former life than anyone had ever been, including those librarians, and now all of that had been packed into Joe's grave (actually, Parsifal wasn't sure if he'd been buried or cremated) along with him.

The memorial service was held in Community Room Number Three of the County Mental Health Service Center, a place done up in soothing pastels, with a blue-grayish plastic folding screen that could be pulled across the center of the room to make the space more intimate if the crowd gathered there was too small, as was the case that morning. Parsifal sat on one of the folding chairs that had been set up ahead of time and sipped from a paper cup of hazelnut-flavored coffee that he had squeezed from a coffee urn on one of the side tables. At the front of the room, a lectern had been placed to give Joe's guests a chance to say a few words about him.

Among the twelve to fifteen people present, somewhat to his surprise, Parsifal appeared to have been Joe's only actual patient at the time of his death. The rest of the group was made up of two ex-wives, a fully grown son, a few colleagues, and one or two others, maybe neighbors. Joe's fellow therapists, distinguished by sport jackets and sweaters atop the men, and by scarves and large rings adorning the women, seemed mostly to be enjoying themselves, criticizing not only the room and the refreshments (sugar cookies with red sprinkles) but also everyone in attendance, taking advantage of Joe's passing as a brief holiday from empathy.

According to the other therapists, Joe had been a maverick in a profession that seemed to attract mavericks. They whispered loudly that if it weren't for the court-appointed cases sent his way by a friendly judge or two, Joe would have had no cases at all. It made Parsifal feel good to know he had been of some use.

The first person to the lectern was a man who introduced himself as Buster. His thin black hair was pulled over his scalp, and he said he'd cut himself shaving that morning, which was why there were pieces of toilet paper stuck to his face. "Bear with me," Buster said. Buster said that he lived in the apartment next door to Joe, and told the group how Joe used to sit up late into the night listening to jazz. Joe favored swing and be-bop, Buster said, and didn't much care for the so-called "progressive" style, but Joe had once admitted to Buster that people had a right to do it, if it meant actual progress.

"That's what I told him," Buster said. "That's exactly what it means."

Buster sat down and was followed by a blond woman in dark glasses whose name Parsifal didn't catch. She'd obviously been crying, and managed only to sob out, "He was so kind and a great tipper," before she sat down again.

Then came a long and awkward silence as the master of ceremonies (Parsifal didn't quite know what to call him) asked if anyone else wanted to speak. Parsifal waited—he was only a patient—*the* patient, it appeared—but after the family waved their arms in the negative to indicate they were too grief-stricken to say anything, and really, they had only come to hear what others had to say about him, and then the other therapists did the same, indicating that whatever they had to offer would more likely come under the heading of professional development than grief, Parsifal felt he had to do something.

Come on, Parsifal, he told himself. *Joe sat through many a missed session and many an hour of listening to you, and when you skipped your appointments because you either forgot, or had better things to do, did he turn you in, as he could have, for being in violation of the terms of your probation? He did not. Did Joe ever so much as raise a hand against you? Most assuredly, he did not.* So Parsifal walked to the lectern, and as he did, heard a small gasp come from the audience. He had no idea of what he was going to say, but the important thing was to fill the silence, to say something. He looked out at the audience and they looked back at him.

"My name is Parsifal," he said. "I am here as a former patient of Joe's, and I just want to tell everyone how sorry I am that Joe stepped into that pit the plumbers had dug outside his door without him knowing anything about it. He was more than a therapist to me; he was also, though he may have denied it, a father figure—and a customer, too, because I once fixed an old Esterbrook he had found in the drawer of his desk. Among inexpensive fountain pens, Esterbrooks are some of the most reliable you can have, in my experience, and if any of you need your fountain pens repaired in the future, I'll be happy to give you a ten percent discount in his memory."

Parsifal sat down, feeling better, and everyone went home soon after that.

The following day Parsifal walked and dragged himself and crawled along the forest floor, over streams and under logs, through early Devonian ferns and mosses, beneath the conifers of the Permian Age, over the grasses of the Eocene, amid the flowering plants of the Paleocene and the occasional contemporary smashed beer can or candy wrapper. (How he missed those energy bars!) He passed a family of deer grazing quietly in a meadow; they looked up with curiosity and, sensing no harm, went back to feeding. He passed a fox playing with her pup, an opossum followed by her brood of baby opossums, fresh out of the pouch; he walked beneath a nest of birds, the small ones stretching out their necks, beaks open wide to receive food from their mother and father; he staggered through a swarm of gnats. It seemed to be family day in the forest, and Parsifal felt strangely sad. Could Walter have been right when he called Parsifal some kind of victim? How could that be, if he himself didn't know?

Parsifal struggled onward, and meanwhile, overhead, the bird was back. He saw no tree with three anchors on its trunk, no door, no cup. He saw nothing but forest and more forest. "No forest goes on forever," is one of the major rules of woodcraft, but Parsifal was starting to doubt it, and to make matters worse, something was happening with his vision. It seemed to be—though he couldn't be absolutely sure—that he was losing the vertical viewing area of his gaze. That is, if his eyes were windows, someone was simultaneously pulling down a set of blinds from the top of the window and raising another set from the bottom. Things were turning into wide-screen mode.

Also, the throbbing in his leg was moving upward, above his knee, but on the positive side, intense pain had a way of pushing aside panic.

Parsifal still had the stone and the shovel, true—but honestly, neither of them was doing him a whole lot of good at that very moment.

Blindness.

During the first years of fountain pens, prior to the actual Golden Age, which was roughly from 1910 to 1950—prior to the invention of the ballpoint, in other words—it is a little known fact that no fountain pen came with the small clip that holds it snugly inside a pocket of a shirt. That was invented by George Parker, of the Parker Pen Company, and ever since then it's hard to imagine a pen without one (though some pens are still made this way, primarily for the Japanese market).

So it *is* possible for something to come from nothing: no clip for many years, and then, suddenly, a clip.

And now, with the fountain pen practically extinct, the clip lives on, attached to ballpoints, and roller balls, and mechanical pencils, and laser pointers.

Did Parsifal hear voices in the distance?

He did not.

All silence the same silence.

Then Parsifal crawled, walked, dragged, et cetera, and once in a while hopped on one foot, too, until, leaning against a tree to catch his breath, his mind was suddenly transfixed by a terrifying sound: the sound of a wrought-iron garden bench, with its legs in the shape of branches and its back made out of metal leaves, whooshing, turning, howling, screaming, end over end and sideways, smashing through the real leaves and branches of the vine-encrusted oak right in front of him.

So much for a truce in the war between the sky and the earth. So much for anything ever getting better. So much for an end to the endless cycle of destruction and being destroyed, of hatred, and revenge, and pride, and fear. Because far from it being some sort of blemish on the face of the world, Parsifal now realized that he had gotten the whole idea wrong. War wasn't the answer; it was the entire game plan. Destruction and violence wasn't the aberration, but the norm, the very axis on which the world was poised. These so-called negative elements were not merely dissonant sparks from the fire of goodness burning somewhere; they weren't sparks at all, but the molten core of things itself. Things falling; things going up in smoke—this was the mechanism, the motor that turned the wheels of the vast and mindless world. Maybe it wasn't revenge at all, or hatred, or any of the names that our puny human vocabularies could bestow on this destruction; maybe it was more like inhaling and exhaling.

The sky wasn't angry for any particular reason, nor was the earth getting even. It was just the way things were.

The falling bench had knocked away the vines in front of the tree, revealing the faint shapes of three anchors carved into its bark long ago, swollen and obscured by time.

The house had been spared by the fire. If Pearl had just stayed home, instead of insisting that she accompany him to the edge of the forest, she probably would have been fine, except for a little smoke inhalation.

All songs the one song.

Nor should it come as a surprise that in days of old the citizens of any society should have striven to expel all monsters, even if there was only a single one. The people looked at the monster and the monster looked back at them, swooping down from time to time to lay waste their towns and fields or to terrorize their virgins. But other than that, the monster always lived alone, in a cave or in a forest out of town, to be sought out as a test of some kind by only the bravest and most foolish of the town's young men. And so the function of the monster was to give mankind a way, however false, to measure its so-called success.

So there Parsifal was, standing outside his own history, looking in at the house where his mother had lived and where he had been raised, and for a few moments he was unable to enter it. What kind of a monster was he to his own past? He looked in and recognized nothing. There were no chairs, no pots and pans, no table, no bed of leaves. It was obvious: it had been decades since he had seen it last, and during those years someone—maybe the same person who had carried away the door (he never really thought that it could have been eaten by an animal, even a porcupine)—had taken everything. He felt more alone than ever—far more alone than when he began the search. And how long ago was that? Parsifal couldn't quite remember.

He had read in a book that in the Triassic Period over

ninety-five percent of all life on this planet was made extinct.

Ninety-five percent of *all* life.

All books the same book.

All sight only a form of blindness.

Which is not to say Parsifal did not search. When he did finally get the nerve to half walk, half crawl into what had once been his home, he looked through everything—turned over every branch and log, swept up every leaf, and even used the shovel he'd found to dig where the floor used to be in hopes of finding something.

It took a while.

And when it came down to it, as tired as he was, and hungry and thirsty—his water was long gone—Parsifal would have settled for any personal item at all to prove that his trip had not been wasted, no matter how pathetic: it was not just Fenjewla that had been his reason for going, it could even be a button, or a bottle, a spoon—*anything* to prove that his past had been more than a dream. But there was nothing—no plate, no pot, no pan; the whole place had been picked absolutely bare, probably by one of those same human vultures who roam the beaches and parks (and, yes, sometimes the forests) with their metal detectors and their baseball caps and their headphones and their trowels in little holsters. But whoever it was, whether one or several people, the place had been completely stripped.

It meant that someone else had the cup.

Or Fenjewla was lost.

It was getting dark again. While Parsifal had pawed through the scraps of his old home, searching for the remains of what had once been his life, he had not felt the pain in his leg, but now that he noticed it again, it had reached his hip, and was two, three, four times worse than ever. Parsifal felt his forehead. It was wet with sweat, not so much from the heat—the air was beginning to cool—but from the exertion and the pain.

It seemed as good a place as any to spend the night.

Had the past been only a dream?

All rain the same rain.

A pen is. And so, *was* it very odd after all for a person to be fond of a sturdy pen that never grows limp in one's hand, never runs out (if you have the kind of pen with an ink window so you can check it) of ink? Certainly, the analogy was nearly embarrassingly transparent, but did that make it less true? And at least it was not that old male/female hobby horse of the cumbersome and completely sterile baseball bat and the first baseman's leather mitt smelling of sweat and neat's-foot oil, or the stubby pigskin of professional football that finds itself tumbling end over end between the upright legs of two spindly goalposts, or the spermlike puck that travels across the ice at lightning speed to be caught inside the waiting net. Or even a hobby horse and rider. No, the notion of a pen as a *fountain* surely must speak volumes.

And so *a pen is*. And if pens *are* that (for who's to say they aren't?), at least their goal is not just to fill the white space of a single waiting piece of paper, or the larger, but still limited area of a human body's skin, but *a pen is* available for projects both large and small, from dotting an *i* to the fourteen syllables of a haiku to a story, a novella, a novel, even a series of novels, a trilogy, with its ink never ceasing to flow (except to pause for refills from a waiting bottle, or several bottles), its nib never changing; just an occasional wipe of the tip and flush of its chamber and *the pen is* ready to continue its own blind and tireless process of production and reproduction: infinite, myriad, endless.

A pen is, and is it any wonder therefore that the rise of women's literature was more or less paralleled by the extinction of the fountain pen, first seeing itself edged to one side by the hard rubber rollers and implacable keys of the typewriter, which was followed by the paperless e-mail wafting across cyberspace like an invisible mist of l'Air du Temps.

But Parsifal was not a writer. Until that moment it had been his job only to *repair* fountain pens, and, like those piano tuners who are able to unleash a burst of Lizst or Rachmaninoff to test the soundboard of a baby grand, and then fall into an embarrassed silence, in Parsifal's profession all he was able to do was to execute a few well-flourished letters, just one sentence:

𝕬𝖑𝖑 𝖙𝖍𝖎𝖓𝖌𝖘 𝖈𝖔𝖒𝖊 𝖙𝖔 𝖙𝖍𝖔𝖘𝖊 𝖜𝖍𝖔 𝖜𝖆𝖎𝖙.

And he had waited. Parsifal had waited for Pearl to see him again in the forest, and waited for Conrad to appear in the city and take his son by his hand and get him a job in a stockbroker's office. He had waited for librarians to finish their interminable shifts, for Joe to change his mind and call him back into his office for one more session, and he had waited for Misty to come to pick up her fountain pen, and he was waiting still.

All journeys the same journey.

A pen is.

So he had been a fool. Parsifal understood that finally, but was there anything he could have done to prevent it? Was there one single act that might have changed him into someone else—not a fool, for example— something he might have done that might have produced a different outcome?

And love? Would that have saved him? If, along the way, he had not been distracted by the informational and recreational aspects of all those librarians, would he have found a different path? Could he still?

He doubted it.

All librarians the same librarian.

And then Parsifal must have passed out for a moment, because when he woke the bird was sitting on a branch above him. And yes, it *was* a bird and not a pilotless drone and not some sort of hallucination, either.

The bird was real, and it resembled a kind of seagull,

but not a seagull exactly. Not an albatross. Not a kestrel. Definitely not an eagle. But what a bird like this one, a seabird—of that he was pretty sure—was doing so far from the ocean he couldn't say. Parsifal wondered if, by any chance, it was lost, but it didn't seem panicked or upset in the least. If anything, it looked benign, its bright eye fixed on him as if it were somehow proud of what he'd done (what *had* he done?), that he'd gotten this far, however far that was, and now the bird was happy to be a witness.

Parsifal studied the bird more closely. It had curved feet, but not those of a predator, a hawk or an eagle, because there was webbing too, and it was a cross between a seabird and a goose, maybe, but it was smaller than a goose, and its feathers were a mix of brown and gray and white, with just a few flecks of yellow here and there, mostly on its breast and neck.

As he looked at the bird, it was clear that it was looking back at him, and its gaze, if anything, was maternal, or possibly paternal—it was hard to tell the sex of birds. "You have done a great job, Parsifal," the bird seemed to be saying. "You have completely surpassed the level of my expectations. I've been keeping an eye on you as best as I could, what with cloud cover and night and so on, and you've gotten much farther than I ever guessed you would. Therefore if I were a betting bird, and had actually made a wager with someone, maybe another bird, I would have to turn to that other bird at this point and tell them I had lost. Congratulations. You really did find your old home, after all. And true, I know you're in pain, but you did well, Parsifal. You did exactly what you were supposed to do."

In actuality, of course, it was hard to tell the bird's expression during all of this due to the more or less solid nature of its beak, which was a deep, though not bright, yellow, and which prevented it from giving off human-based emotion-indicators such as a smile, or frown, or a grimace. But there *was* something encouraging in the way the bird would tilt its head one way and then tilt it in another, a completely different direction—something jaunty, jocular, and even curiously intimate. It gave Parsifal a good feeling. Also, the bird seemed to be patient as well, and not at all as restless as a human might be under such circumstances. Nor was it lifting first one foot and then the other as he had seen parrots in cages do.

Parsifal looked to see if, by any chance, there might be a tiny camera mounted on one of its legs or maybe between its wings, so that someone might be looking at him right then, writing down the coordinates and calling up a Search and Rescue team, but his eyes seemed to have gotten even worse, and he was having real trouble seeing.

Parsifal listened for voices, but all he could hear was his own heart beating in his ears.

After a lifetime, what fragments remain? Pearl, Conrad, Parsifal.

Make sure that all fires are dead out.

The silence of a falling star
Lights up a purple sky

A pen is.

All pens the same pen.

And as I wonder where you are

It was getting cold, and Parsifal remembered his early lessons in woodcraft: If a person is caught in the woods at night and there's not a cliff to hide behind to stop the wind and no cave to crawl into (and at that moment there was neither), the best thing to do to keep warm is to scoop a shallow cup out of the earth—not so deep that the ground beneath a person is cold or wet, and not so large as not to contain the heat. Then lie down in it and wait for the morning.

I'm so lonesome

Make sure that all fires are dead out.

I'm so lonesome

Parsifal looked in his backpack once again to see if by any chance he had overlooked any energy bars or packs of matches. He hadn't.

Cody. Joe. Geronimo. George Armstrong Custer. Fenjewla. Misty.

I could cry

All names the same name.

Cuplike.

All cups the same cup.

And where was that shovel, anyway?

Using his hands Parsifal dug out a shallow circle, shoveled leaves down into the bottom, and then put his sleeping bag on top. He unzipped the bag and dragged his legs inside, then zipped it shut again to make the coldness go away. He was hungry, but eating would have to wait, and he was thirsty, too, his mouth dry, uncomfortable. He remembered from his woodcraft book that if this sort of situation should arise, the best thing was to find a small stone or a pebble and to hold it in one's mouth.

All time the same time.

Blindness the same blindness.

Parsifal shut his eyes and reached into his pocket, where he found Black Dog's pebble. He put it in his mouth and felt better. He closed his eyes and pulled the bag up to his chin. Both his legs were completely numb, so at least the pain had finally disappeared. *Not bad*, he thought. *Not bad at all.* Maybe he would dream, and maybe he wouldn't; he didn't know what would happen next. Above him was the sky; below him was the earth.

Fenjewla.

All doors the same door.

And so, he thought, *tomorrow was another day—or something.*

My thanks as always to all the people at Tin House Books, and especially Lee Montgomery, whose generous and perceptive editing vastly improved this book. Thanks as well to Janice Shapiro, whose early reading shaped the manuscript's form, and to Monana Wali, who helped refine it. As always, this book could not have been finished without the support of my wife, Jenny.